The ghost appears. . . .

Without breaking the circle, I turned my head. About halfway down the aisle that ran between the rows of pews, a mist was forming. Swirling. Growing thicker. Harlan's fingers tightened on my hand until I swear I could hear bones crunching.

"Moses, is that you?" Lara asked.

"No," a voice answered. High and squeaky. It didn't sound human.

"Can you tell us who you are?" Lara asked.

"I don't remember." It was kind of like listening to a rusty door hinge talking.

"Were you a patient at the Undercliff Asylum?" Lara continued.

"I don't remember."

"What do you remember?" asked Lara.

"Someone hurt me," the spirit squealed. "Someone hurt me," it repeated, and the sound of its voice changed, became lower, softer. Human. Female.

Across the circle from me, Danny's eyes went wide. I jerked my head back toward the mist. Something was moving in it now. Forming.

Blond hair. Pale face. A girl. About my age. A dress blowing around her l⬛⬛⬛⬛⬛⬛⬛⬛⬛⬛body hurt me," she said.

And Cyndi scream⬛⬛⬛⬛⬛⬛⬛⬛⬛⬛ the walls of the chapel. "I⬛⬛⬛⬛⬛⬛⬛⬛⬛⬛Get her away from me! Pl⬛⬛⬛⬛⬛⬛⬛⬛away from me!"

THE HARDY BOYS

Undercover Brothers®

Available from Simon & Schuster

THE

HARDY BOYS

Undercover Brothers®

FRANKLIN W. DIXON

#24 **HAUNTED**

SPECIAL GHOST STORIES EDITION

Aladdin Paperbacks

New York   London   Toronto   Sydney

This book is a work of fiction. Any references to historical events, real people, or real locales are used fictitiously. Other names, characters, places, and incidents are the product of the author's imagination, and any resemblance to actual events or locales or persons, living or dead, is entirely coincidental.

ALADDIN PAPERBACKS
An imprint of Simon & Schuster Children's Publishing Division
1230 Avenue of the Americas, New York, NY 10020
Copyright © 2008 by Simon & Schuster, Inc.
All rights reserved, including the right of reproduction in whole or in part
in any form.
ALADDIN PAPERBACKS , THE HARDY BOYS MYSTERY STORIES,
HARDY BOYS UNDERCOVER BROTHERS, and related logo
are registered trademarks of Simon & Schuster, Inc.
Designed by Sammy Yuen
The text of this book was set in Aldine 401 BT.
Manufactured in the United States of America
First Aladdin Paperbacks edition August 2008
10 9 8 7 6 5 4 3 2 1
Library of Congress Control Number 2008920168
ISBN-13: 978-1-4169-6169-7
ISBN-10: 1-4169-6169-0

TABLE OF CONTENTS

JOE

1

Implosion!

"They want us to get off at that platform," I told Frank.

"The platform's abandoned," Frank said. Sometimes Frank has this thing where he has to state what is totally obvious. "The train's not stopping there."

I double-checked the text that had just been zapped to my phone. "That's where they want us to make the drop." A new text appeared. I showed the message to Frank. TICK-TOCK. TOBY DOESN'T HAVE MUCH TIME.

I couldn't even see the section of old platform anymore. We'd already gone past it. Frank leaped up and headed for the back of our car, grabbing a couple of newspapers that had been left lying on the seats. I was pretty sure I knew what he had planned. If I was right, I was very sure I wasn't going to like it.

He opened the door and stepped out on the metal slats between the subway cars. "We're going to have to jump."

"Dude, I want to get the money to the kidnappers. But we have to be going seventy miles an hour. How are we supposed to walk back to that platform if we're deceased?"

"There's a curve coming up. The train will have to slow down, probably to about thirty," Frank answered. He crumpled up some of the newspaper and stuffed it under his sweater sleeves to pad his elbows.

He handed one of the newspapers to me, and I crumpled and stuffed sheets of it everywhere possible. I would have swallowed some if I thought that would protect me from possible internal injuries.

"Okay, here it comes. We're slowing down. Jump perpendicular to the train," Frank advised.

"Oh, you want me to jump *away* from the train, not toward it?" I muttered. I get kind of sarcastic when I'm freaked out of my head. But Frank was right. Toby's kidnappers weren't exactly patient. We didn't have time to get to the next stop and work our way back.

The brakes squealed a little as the train slowed.

"Now or never," said Frank. And he jumped.

I pressed my tongue to the roof of my mouth. I hate biting my tongue. Did a check for anything big and hard in my path—as well as I could in the darkness of the subway tunnel. Then crouched down, covered my head with my arms, and jumped.

Roll like a log, I told myself in the second before the splat. It's better to let your whole body absorb the impact instead of just one or two parts.

Wham! I guess I did the landing correctly, because every single inch of my body was feeling the pain. I staggered to my feet and sucked in a deep breath. "You survive?" Frank called to me.

"Yeah." I walked toward him, pulling out my newspaper stuffing. He flicked on one of his thin, super-high-power flashlights. Standard ATAC issue. That's American Teens Against Crime. Frank and I are two of the American teens. We'd been recruited to the agency because our dad helped found it. He figured—and he was right—that there are some situations where teenagers make the best undercover ops.

I like to think the ATAC talent scouts would have found us on their own. Frank and I do have a reputation in Bayport as amateur detectives.

"Remind me to send an e-mail to ATAC asking them for crash-landing pads that can be instantly inflated. And they should be no bigger than a dollar bill when flat."

Frank snorted. "Okay, James Bond."

You know what? Frank gets a little sarcastic too sometimes. Like when he's bleeding.

"Are you all right?" I asked him. "There's blood coming out of your mouth."

"Bit my tongue," he answered as he led the way back to the old platform.

I saw the words SCOLLY-BRATTLE LOOP painted on one of the walls. "Oh, man. I saw this special on albino underground dwellers, and the Scolly-Brattle loop is where they lived. They were albino because they'd lived down here for generations, ever since this cave-in. They're supposed to have gills even, because it's always so—"

"I'm getting you the Weemote," Frank interrupted. "You clearly can't handle viewing all the channels. I'm blocking everything but CNN and PBS."

"That albino underground dwellers special was on PBS," I told him. "Hey, there it is. The platform. At least they kept the juice on." A row of steel-shaded lamps hung from the ceiling. They gave out some weak light.

"Don't see anybody," said Frank. "Do they think we're just going to drop the money without getting Toby first?"

That's Toby Allison. Yeah, that Toby Allison. The skateboarding guru. Someone made an attempt to kidnap him a week ago, so ATAC assigned us to go undercover as part of his crew. There were always a bunch of skateboarders hanging out with Toby. The kidnappers managed to grab him again. Part of their demands was that the ransom be delivered by two members of Toby's entourage. No cops. No FBI. Just kids who had been seen with Toby.

Frank and I made sure we were the kids who were going to do the ransom drop. But where were the kidnappers? And Toby?

I hauled myself up onto the platform, wishing I'd left my newspaper stuffing in place. Frank climbed up next to me. I scanned the area. Cement floor. Red columns. An old pay phone. Benches. A couple of big wire trash cans. Some rats. No humans in sight.

I turned in a slow circle. I wanted to make sure I hadn't missed anything. Then the pay phone began to ring.

"There's no way that thing should be working," said Frank.

"I guess our kidnappers have some skillz," I answered.

Frank picked up the phone. "We're here," he said into the receiver. He listened for a moment. "We're not leaving the money until we see Toby." He listened for another moment, then turned to me. "Check your cell."

I pulled out the phone. It had a thin crack across the video screen, but it was working. "What am I looking for?" I asked Frank.

Before he could answer, a video clip began to play. A clip of me and Frank standing on the deserted platform. I lifted one hand in a wave. The little Joe on the screen did too. "We're under live surveillance," I told Frank.

The screen went blank for a second, then a new image came up. Toby. Tied up inside a large, empty room. "Lee, Erik, it's me." Lee and Erik were Frank's and my aliases for the mission. "It's Friday at ten thirty-three. I'm okay. Just do whatever they say."

The camera on Toby pulled back. Back and back until we could see the outside of the ten-story building. And the street signs at the corner.

"They're saying the building is scheduled for demolition in ten minutes," Frank said. "If we leave now, we'll have time to get Toby out. They'll unlock the door leading to the stairway out of here if they see us leave the cash."

I rushed over to the door. Tried it. Locked. "We have no way to know that they're not messing with our heads."

I heard the sound of an explosion and jerked up my cell. A section of the building that Toby was being held in had just been blown away.

Frank and I looked at each other. He took off his backpack and unzipped it. He held it open wide, showing the stacks and stacks of hundred-dollar bills. Then he put the backpack down and joined me at the door.

I tried it again. And it opened.

I hit speed dial 1 and got Vijay Patel on the phone as we took the stairs. Vijay handles a lot of the tech stuff for us when we're in the field. He wants to be a field op himself, and I'm betting he will be pretty fast.

"Vijay, we need the fastest route from—" I checked the street signs and gave him our location and the location of the building where Toby was being held. Vijay rattled off directions, and Frank and I ran. Our feet were the fastest way there.

The kidnappers were dead-on with the calculations. We raced up to the building eight and a half minutes later. That gave us a minute and a half to get Toby out of there. We should just be able to make it—but there definitely wasn't any time to spare. The non-load-bearing walls had already been removed. That would make the building go down faster.

"Let's split up to do the search," I suggested.

"I'll take—"

Bwam!

The floor bucked underneath my feet, and my ears rang with the sound of the blast.

"They've started the demolition!" Frank yelled, choking on the cloud of dust the explosion had sent into the air.

"They never expected us to get Toby out!" I shouted back.

"That blast was localized. Just the bottom of the center row of columns, I think," said Frank. "They should go for the bottom of the side columns next. Then somewhere near the tops of all the columns with the third blast."

If we were inside for the third blast, we'd be demolished along with the building. "I'll go left, you go right," I barked. Then I took off for the columns I knew had to be supporting my side of the building.

With most of the walls gone, it wasn't hard to find the columns I was looking for.

Bore holes. That's what I needed. Blasters drill holes into the cement of the columns and stuff them full of dynamite or other explosive stuff. When the combustible chemical or whatever the explosive is burns, it creates a huge amount of gas in a super-short amount of time. The pressure builds, then—*kablam!*

All right. There was one of those beautiful holes. Loops of yellow and green wire spilled out of it. I ran my fingers over them. They were cool.

Good sign. The wires were basically the fuse. The end of the wires would be surrounded by a small amount of explosive material. The heat from an electrical current running through the wires would cause a small explosion when it reached the material. And this would set off the primer charge that would set off the *kablam*.

So I had to stop the heat. I pulled my Swiss Army knife out of my pocket. Cut the wires, stop the heat, right? I hoped so. I positioned the knife under a section of both the yellow and green wire, and cut them both at the same moment.

Nothing exploded. I wasn't positive nothing would explode, but there were two more columns with bore holes full of explosives to deal with. I dashed to the next column. Grabbed a yellow wire and a green wire. Hot. They were hot.

Bad sign. So bad. I slashed them. No *kablam*. I took off toward the last column, and—you got it—*kablam*. I was suddenly flying away from the column. Off my feet flying.

I hit the ground hard. *I really should just wear padding at all times,* I thought as small pieces of cement slammed into me like BBs from a BB gun. But at least the building didn't come crashing down on me.

I scrambled to my feet and saw Frank running toward me. "You saved two columns. Great. Me too. I don't think we're going to be able to get to the tops of the columns before they blow. Let's just find Toby and hope what we did is enough to keep the building standing."

Hope. Yeah. I was hoping big-time.

Frank and I found the stairs and took them as fast as we could. No Toby on the second floor.

We started for the third. *Kablam!*

The building rocked. It sounded like the tops of all the columns had been detonated together. But the bottoms of four of those columns were solid. They had to hold. Well, they didn't really *have* to, but I figured the power of positive thinking couldn't hurt.

No Toby on the third floor.

No Toby on the fourth.

On the fifth, we heard him screaming.

Frank untied his feet. I untied his hands. "Hope you're as fast off a board as on," I told him.

He ran for the stairs. Good answer.

Frank and I were right behind him.

I could hear the building groaning. *Hold on a little longer*, I begged silently.

The building shuddered as we hit the second floor. *Just a little longer.*

We reached the first floor and tore out the front door. A few seconds later a cloud of dust surrounded us. The dust blinded me. It filled my nose and lungs, choking me.

When it cleared, the building was gone.

Imploded!

"We were supposed to be under there," Frank said, staring at the pile of rubble.

"But we're not," I answered. I turned to Toby. "Any chance you can ID the people who snatched you? Since you're alive and everything."

Toby grinned. "Absolutely."

Frank grinned too. "That means that the kidnappers better watch their backs. Starting right now."

Autopsy Report

"**H**eads up!" Joe yelled.

I jerked my head up, looking for something to catch. A zombie was flying at me, an ax still in its forehead. Green drool flying out of its mouth.

Not catchable.

I threw myself to the ground. The zombie flew over me, the feet of its size-thirteen work boots skimming over my back. "That was definitely a 'hit the floor' moment, not a 'heads up,'" I told Joe as I shoved myself to my feet. "And why was that zombie flying? Zombies don't fly."

"Zombies don't exist at all. The dead cannot extract energy from consuming gray matter and use it to propel themselves forward in any manner," Joe answered, doing what he thinks is a hilarious impression of me. "And anyway," he added, dropping his Frank thing, "this is a haunted house we're building. It's a place where anything can happen."

Joe walked over to the zombie and studied it. "The plastic trick-or-treating pumpkin you added doesn't really work for me. Unless—were you planning to fill it with brains? Because that would be cool."

"I didn't put the pumpkin in its hand," I answered. "Chet and I've been working on plugging up the leaks in the swamp. I came over to tell you it's ready for that other creature you made—if you're sure it's waterproof."

"Definitely. Help me carry it. It's on the loading dock. I was letting the coat of sealant dry out there," Joe told me. He grabbed the plastic pumpkin out of the ghost-zombie's hand as we passed it. Something rattled inside.

Joe froze and peered into the pumpkin. "It's go time," he told me. He tilted the pumpkin so I could see the video game disc inside. Or what looked like a video game disc. That's how our missions from ATAC are delivered to us.

"Let's still go to the loading dock. We can watch it out there," I suggested. We'd gotten permission to use a building that used to be a grocery store for the haunted house. It was up for sale and wasn't being used for anything. Plus the haunted house was for UNICEF, which made people want to help us out.

The loading dock was empty, just like I'd figured. When we got out there, Joe snapped the disc into his portable game player. The photo of a laughing teenage girl filled the screen. *"This is Maryama Soll,"* the voice of our ATAC contact began. *"She was sentenced to a six-week stay at the Undercliff House of Detention in Glastonbury, Connecticut, after repeated incidents of shoplifting. She never made it out of the detention center. Before the six weeks were up, Maryama died there.*

"The coroner was unable to determine the cause of death." Maryama's picture was replaced on the screen by her autopsy report. *"She seemed to be in good health and free from obvious trauma or toxins. However, her blood work showed unusually high amounts of adrenaline and CRH—the brain's hypothalamic stress hormone. In an off-the-record comment to a homicide detective, the coroner stated that it was almost as if Maryama had been frightened to death."*

The autopsy report faded, and one of Maryama's autopsy photos took its place. "Whoa," Joe whispered. My stomach did a slow roll in my belly. Maryama didn't look anything like the laughing girl in the first picture anymore. Her face was frozen in an expression of total terror, her mouth open in what looked like a scream, her eyes open so wide you could see the whites all the way around her irises.

The autopsy report of Gregory Teeter was very similar. No obvious cause of death. High amounts of adrenaline and CRH. A newspaper photo of a serious-looking boy flashed on the screen, quickly followed by a photo of the same boy on an autopsy table, his face twisted into a grimace.

"There are rumors among the teens living at the Under-cliff House of Detention that the place is haunted," our contact went on. A video clip of a bunch of kids playing soccer in front of a huge stone building appeared on the screen. Undercliff, obviously. I don't believe in ghosts. But if I did, that heap of gray stone looked like exactly the kind of place a ghost would live. Afterlive? *"Even some of the people living in Glastonbury seem to believe there is something evil about the place. The rumors may have had their start in Undercliff's history. When it was built in 1794, it was used as an insane asylum, and many of the patients there were badly mistreated."*

"That's exactly the kind of place that would be haunted," Joe said. "A place where there's been a lot of pain."

"Joe, that's not—," I began. I didn't have to tell him that ATAC wasn't giving us the assignment of dealing with ghosts. Our contact did it for me. *"Clearly, there is a rational explanation for the deaths of Maryama Soll and Gregory Teeter,"* he said as the video clip continued to play. *"Your mission is to find out who is responsible for their deaths."*

My eyes locked on all those kids playing soccer. Joe and I needed to work fast. We had to find out what was really going on at Undercliff before one of them ended up dead too.

The screen went blank. If we tried to play it again, it would probably blast out a Jessica Simpson song. We got only one chance to watch our mission assignment, for security reasons. "Anything else in the pumpkin?" I asked Joe.

"Some undercover background info for us," he answered. "Train tickets. And this." He pulled out a worn piece of paper. "It says it was in Maryama's pocket when she died."

Wednesday, March 14, 1810
I keep my mind on happy moments. A walk by the lake with the dogs. I see a nest with a wren on it. I eat leaning against a stone wall. A night dining at the home of Mr. Werry. Chess afterward. A day with a letter from Charlotte. Weeding the turnips, with

my hands in the warm earth. Fishing in moonlight. Lying in my own bed.

But the screams tear the memories from my head. Its never silent here. There is always someone screaming in fear, whether real or imaginary. Does it really matter which? Pain is pain.

I am Moses Bottelle. I do not belong here. I tell myself that again and again. I am Moses Bottelle. I do not belong here. I will not allow myself to become a screaming one. I will go over my happy memories. I will stay sane. I will not scream. I will not become one of them simply because I am surrounded by them.

I will not scream.

JOE
3

Ghost Hunters

The flashlight beam swept across the doll's chalk white face. And when it hit the doll's eyes, the pupils contracted.

I know what you're thinking. *You're thinking, Joe, dolls' eyes are made of plastic. The pupils are painted on.*

 FRANK

Frank here. Just wanted to say that's definitely what I'm thinking. Now I'm leaving. I know this is Joe's section.

 JOE

Well, duh. I know the pupils are painted on. But

they shrunk to pinpoints in the bright light anyway. Just like a living person's would.

I shoveled a piece of blueberry pie into the side of my face. Frank cracked up. "Joe, your mouth is that big open part in the middle of your face," he told me. "That's where the food goes."

Aunt Trudy leaned across the table and snatched my cell phone out of my lap. "Here's the problem," she announced to the rest of the family. "He's trying to watch the doohickey while he's eating." She pulled my dessert plate toward her.

"Hey!" I protested.

"If you're going to eat one of my homemade pies, you're going to give it your full attention," Aunt T said.

I wanted to explain that I had been doing important research. Research that could end up saving my life—and Frank's—on our mission. Every episode of *Spectral*—the TV show detailing the cases of the most successful ghost-hunting team ever—I could watch before Frank and I walked into the Undercliff House of Detention could help us deal with what we might find there.

But I couldn't tell Mom and Aunt Trudy that. They didn't know we were ATAC. The only reason Dad knew was because he founded the organization after he retired. Most agents have to keep the secret from their entire family plus everybody else in their lives.

Mom and Aunt Trudy thought Frank and I were heading to Connecticut with our school science club to check out the fall leaves. That was one of the few parts of being with ATAC that stank. Lying to them. Especially because they would both go into ultrahelpful mode when we were going away. Mom had been giving us all this info on why leaves change color. Like the red in maples is from glucose left over after photosynthesis stops. She's a research librarian, so she knows everything about everything. And Aunt Trudy had already started making sure that we had enough warm socks.

"What is this you were watching?" Aunt Trudy burst out. "It looks like a doll is trying to suck the breath out of a child."

"It's *Spectral*. It's a show about true hauntings," I explained. While her attention was on the phone, I slid my pie back in front of me. Aunt Trudy's blueberry pie is *gooood*.

"Just so you know, it isn't a show that's on CNN," said Frank.

"Do you think it's impossible that ghosts exist, Frank?" Mom asked him.

"Don't you?" he replied.

She gave a half smile. "'There are more things

in heaven and earth, Horatio, than are dreamt of in your philosophy,'" she answered.

"Okay, great Shakespeare quote. But really," Frank said.

"With all the things we know, there are so many things we don't know," Mom explained. "Think of all we've learned about subatomic particles. Who knows what else is beyond what our current technology is able to detect?"

"I'm with you, Mom. But you're freaking Frank out," I told her.

"I'm not freaked out," Frank said quickly. "I'm just surprised. Mom's usually so much about the facts." He turned to Dad. "What's your take on ghosts?"

"In all my years as a PI, all the cases I worked on with the police, I never came across anything that couldn't be explained by physical evidence and human motives," Dad answered.

Aunt Trudy managed to turn off the show on my cell. "I figure if I don't believe in ghosts, they won't believe in me. And that's how I like it."

"Wimps! Wimps! Wimps!" Playback commented from his perch in the kitchen. "Merry Christmas! Ho, ho, ho!" Our parrot has a large vocabulary. He picked up some from the perp we rescued him from. Some from our family. And some from so-called friends. The "wimps, wimps, wimps" thing came from Brian Conrad. And yeah, he was talking about me and Frank.

"I have some extra homework to do." Frank ate his last bite of pie. "Stuff that has to be finished before the trip."

Translation: We needed to prep for our mission.

"Yeah, me too," I said.

We cleared the table, loaded the dishwasher, then headed up to Frank's room. Frank avoids my room as much as possible. He's afraid he'll catch something in there. I keep telling him that it's actually good for your immune system to be exposed to some dirt, but he doesn't go for it. And he's supposed to be a science head.

I sat down in front of Frank's computer and got another episode of *Spectral* going.

"Joe, enough. We need to get our cover stories down," Frank told me.

"We also need as much ghost-hunting information as possible," I reminded him. "They're explaining about cold spots right now. We might need to know about them. They're a signal that a ghost is present. That could give us a heads-up at Undercliff."

"There's no ghost at Undercliff." Frank pulled out the fake IDs, police reports, and other background material we'd gotten in the plastic pumpkin.

"Maybe. Maybe not. Anyway, I can multitask.

Hit me," I said, watching a mist curl itself around a house. Just one house out of a whole block.

"You multitask so well, you're lucky you don't have four fork holes straight through your cheek," Frank shot back. "Here's the deal. We're brothers." He glanced at the door. "And we found a way to hack into Auction House."

"That new eBay wannabe site." See. Multitasking.

The ghost hunters were playing back a film of the mist now. And you could see a man in it. So clear.

"We figured out a way to siphon off a small amount—just two cents—of every purchase made on the site." He did another door check.

"We're so . . . freaky," I said. One of the hunters had walked right through the ghost man. "I mean freaky smart," I added quickly so Frank wouldn't realize my attention had drifted for a sec. "We're diabolically clever."

Frank shook his head. "I'm diabolically clever enough to know that you aren't paying enough attention. Shut it off."

"You only want me to shut it off because it's giving you the creeps," I told him.

"Joe, there's no scientific evidence that proves the existence of ghosts," Frank said. "If anyone had actual proof, it would be a massive news story. Bigger than landing on the moon."

"The guys on *Spectral* take electromagnetic readings. They—," I began.

"But how has it ever been determined that ghosts cause electromagnetic fluctuations?" Frank interrupted. "Answer: It hasn't."

"Then why do you keep looking at the door?" I asked. "Admit it. All the ghost talk has gotten you a little nervous." It had gotten me a little nervous. Not that I was going to admit it. "So you have to believe that there's some possibility they exist."

Frank laughed. "I guess I keep looking at the door because I keep expecting Dad to come in. You know he's not going to be able to stop himself from handing out some advice and telling us to be careful."

"Maybe he's finally realized that we've been on a whole bunch of missions and that we actually know what we're doing," I suggested. It was something we'd been trying to gently pound into his head for a while.

"Possible," said Frank. He sounded doubtful. "Anyway. Back to our cover." He gave my chair a push with his foot, and it rolled away from the computer. "Auction House closes about half a million auctions a day."

"So Frank and Joe McClain were getting about

ten grand a day. Nice!" I rolled myself back over to the computer.

"Until they got caught and sentenced to a stay in Undercliff," Frank reminded me.

Frank's computer mooed. "That's your new sound for when you have mail. I set it up for you," I told him. He didn't smile. "You don't find it amoosing?" I asked. He still didn't smile.

When they complete the Human Genome Project, maybe something can be done about Frank's inability to process humor. I vacated the chair and let Frank at the keyboard.

"You won't believe this," he said. "Or actually, maybe you will."

"What?"

"It's from Dad. To both of us," Frank said. He read the e-mail aloud. "'Guys. Just wanted to wish you a safe mission. Undercliff has extremely tight security. You're not going to be able to get out if things get tough. Watch yourselves.'"

"Well, it wasn't a twenty-minute lecture. So he's improving," I commented. "Better delete that e-mail right away."

"Already happening." Frank moved aside so I could see that the message had broken into fragments on its own. The pieces disintegrated, returning the screen to *Spectral*.

Frank snorted as one of the ghost hunters went over a room with a Geiger counter. "If they do get a reading for radiation, what is that supposed to prove?"

I wondered if Frank's opinion on ghosts would change at all after being locked away in a place that was supposed to be haunted.

4

New Meat

Undercliff looked worse than it had on the little screen of Joe's game player. Mostly because it was massive. Two huge slabs of gray stone formed an L shape, with rows of small square windows on the second and third floors. There were fewer windows on the first floor, but they were larger.

"And you wanted to go to Hawaii," Joe joked.

One of the guards escorting us through the security gate—the only part of the place that seemed like it came from this century—snorted. "Wouldn't be surprised if Dr. Beirly throws a luau one night."

"Yeah. If the judges who sentence kids to time here knew half of what goes on at this place . . ."

The other guard shook his head, setting his short ponytail swinging.

Huh. I wouldn't have minded asking the guards some questions, but we'd arrived at the entrance. Snorting Guard shoved open the mammoth wooden door and ushered us inside.

"Here's the new meat," he told the tall, gawky guy waiting for us.

"Thanks," the guy said. "And lay off the prison movies a little, okay? We don't use words like 'meat' here—except to refer to something on a plate. Try some romantic comedies." He winked. "It'll get you more chicks."

Ponytail Guard just shoved some papers at him in response. "I'm Micah Neel, by the way," the tall guy told me and Joe as he signed. "I do a little of everything around here." He handed the papers back, and the guards headed off.

"Bye, guys!" Micah called after the closed door. "Good to see you again!" He shrugged. "They work for the city. We haven't exactly bonded. So, Frank and Joe McClain. Which one's Frank and which one's Joe?"

We introduced ourselves, and Micah led us up a wide staircase for two floors, and then down a long hall. The inside of the building was nothing like the outside. The walls were a soft peach color. I suspected it was a color that psychologists had determined kept people calm and happy. A light beige carpet covered the floor. And there were some hotel-room kind of paintings around—flowers, a sailboat on a still blue sea, a sunset.

"The first thing you gotta do is have an intake interview with Dr. Beirly. He's the man. The guy in charge of the place," Micah told us as he led the way into your basic waiting room. "You go in first, Frank. Right through that door."

I was expecting an office, but it was like walking into somebody's living room. A large, doughy man stood up from the sofa and shook my hand. "Elton Beirly," he said. "Have a seat."

I grabbed the nearest chair, wondering what Beirly's approach was going to be. The last time Joe and I had gone undercover at a juvenile detention center was nothing like this. That one was out in the woods, and the guy in charge had started barking orders at us the second we'd arrived.

"I just want to take a few minutes to find out a little about you," Beirly went on. "What you like and don't like." He smiled. "I'm guessing you like computers, seeing what you're in here for."

I shifted uncomfortably in my seat, not quite meeting his eyes. I figured that's how Frank McClain would respond. "Yeah, I guess," I muttered.

"You'd have to have put in a lot of hours to hack Auction House," Beirly commented.

He picked a clipboard up from the coffee table. "Okay, I have some questions for you. I'm going to ask them quickly, and I'd like you to answer them quickly. Let's go. Would you rather go white-water rafting or play baseball?"

"Rafting," I answered. I didn't have time to decide if that's what Frank McClain would think or not.

"Would you rather see an action movie or a comedy?"

I hesitated.

"Don't think, just speak," Beirly coached.

"Action."

This was clearly a psychological test. Were my answers going to fit with the answers of a kid who'd gotten arrested for theft? Were there specific answers that a kid who'd committed a crime like "I" had would give? About movies and baseball?

"At an amusement park, would you rather go on a roller coaster or hang in the arcade?" Beirly asked.

"Roller coaster."

And it went on like that. On and on. Would I rather have a snake or a ferret? Go to Rome or India? Skydive or sail? Read Stephen King or *Rolling Stone?* Surf or play beach volleyball?

"That's it," Beirly finally announced.

I felt like I had a ball of mush in my head instead of a brain. My mouth was dry. I must have answered hundreds of questions.

"Is there anything you want to ask me after all that?" said Beirly. "You'll get filled in on the schedule and whatnot as you go on, but feel free to ask anything."

I wasn't going to pass up a chance like that. "I . . . uh . . ." I looked at the floor, then up at Beirly, like I was embarrassed by what I was about to say. "One of the guys at the courthouse, he said this place was haunted."

Beirly nodded. "We can't seem to shake that rumor," he admitted. "Probably because the building is so old, built back in 1794. Most old places have a ghost story or two about them. And you have to admit, Undercliff does look a little spooky."

"Yeah," I agreed. I decided to push a little further. "Is it true it used to be an insane asylum?"

"So you heard that, too?" I nodded, and Beirly sighed. "Yes, it's true. And though the doctors had the best of intentions, some of the treatments they used on their patients would be considered torture today. This wing was used for hydrotherapy. Patients who became hysterical were placed into tubs of ice."

"For how long?" I asked.

"Hours," he answered. "Sometimes even days. It was a terrible thing. It's the patients who were so mistreated here that some people believe haunt the building."

"Have you ever seen anything?" I asked.

"Only once," Beirly said quickly. "But you don't have to worry about that. I recently had a psychic come in and cleanse the place."

"A psychic?"

So Beirly had brought a psychic into Undercliff. And he was very willing to talk about the "hauntings." It was almost like he was encouraging people to think Undercliff had ghosts.

SUSPECT PROFILE

Name: Dr. Elton Beirly

Hometown: Cambridge, Massachusetts

Physical description: 6'3", approximately 280 lbs., age 38, dark brown hair, brown eyes.

Occupation: Director, Undercliff House of Detention

Background: Only child. Father a Nobel Prize-winning scientist. Mother a stay-at-home mom.

Suspicious Behavior: Very willing to talk about ghosts. Perhaps using ghost stories to cover up what really happened to Maryama and Gregory.

"It's not that I'm a believer, exactly. That night I saw—thought I saw—something, I'd been working late and was overtired." Beirly gave a short laugh. "But bringing in the psychic felt like the right thing to do. It felt right to acknowledge the pain that had happened here, all around us."

He stood up and put his hand on my shoulder. "Don't let it keep you up at night, Frank. If there ever were any ghosts at Undercliff, I promise you they're gone now."

Cold Spot

*C*lick-clack-clack. There was that sound again. It was driving me nuts. It wasn't loud or anything, but I couldn't figure out where it was coming from.

Who cares where it's coming from? I asked myself. *It's just a little sound.* I focused my attention on the *Sports Illustrated* again. Make that *tried* to focus my attention.

Click-click-clack.

Wasn't that making Micah crazy too? I looked over at him. He was still working away at his paperwork over at the desk. It was like he didn't even hear it. Maybe it was like the sound of knuckles cracking. It made some people's ears want to shrivel up, but others hardly noticed it.

I tossed the *Sports Illustrated* back on the table in front of me. Whatever Frank and Beirly were talking about was taking a while.

"They should be finishing up pretty soon," Micah told me.

I nodded and jammed my hands into my pockets. "This place must be hard to heat, huh?" I asked.

"Not really." He twisted around and checked the thermostat on the wall behind him. "It's almost seventy. You cold?"

"A little," I answered.

"Well, you're over by the windows. Even though they're closed, that makes a difference. I'll crank it up a little." Micah gave the thermostat knob a twist.

"Thanks." I leaned back in my chair.

Crack-crack-click.

It wasn't just that I couldn't figure out where the sound was coming from that was making me insane. It was that the sound was really familiar, but I couldn't figure out how it was familiar. It was on the tip of my tongue. Or I guess earlobe.

Click-crack-click.

"What's that sound?" I finally burst out.

"I didn't hear anything," Micah answered.

"It's not loud, but it keeps happening. It's a clicking, cracking. It sounds kind of like when you make the break when you're playing pool. But not exactly, and not that loud," I explained.

I pulled the hood of my sweatshirt up. The thermostat had to be wrong. I was getting goose bumps. I decided to move away from the windows. I took two steps, and—

Crack-crack-click.

I knew what the sound was. Ice in a glass. The cubes clicking and cracking against one another. That's exactly what the sound was.

Except there was no ice anywhere around.

Just give it a rest, I told myself. *The building's hundreds of years old. It's just some strange noise the floor or the walls are making.*

I crossed the room and sat in a big armchair. It wasn't much warmer on this side of the room. Make that any warmer.

I wrapped my arms around my chest. I felt like the cold was taking over my body. Turning me into a cube of ice, like the ones I kept thinking I heard.

"Joe!" said Micah sharply. I jerked my head up and saw him rushing toward me. "I think we need to get you out of here."

"Why?" I asked. And I could see my breath.

"Just get up and come on." Micah pulled me to my feet and hustled me into the hall. It felt like walking from a freezer into an oven.

"Do you need a blanket or anything?" Micah asked. "I didn't realize . . . I thought you were just a little cold. You must be really sensitive. Has anything like that ever happened to you before?"

I rubbed my hands together. "Getting cold, you mean?"

"No, I mean . . ." Micah shook his head. "I don't mean anything."

"I can't believe you weren't freezing too," I said. I didn't see one goose bump on Micah. It's like I was in the only cold spot in the room.

Wait. Cold spot. *Cold spot.*

They talked about cold spots on one of the *Spectral* episodes. They were one of the indicators that a house was haunted.

What Are You in For?

"So, do you want to know what I'm in for?" a girl in a lime green hoodie asked me in the lunch line. Joe was still at his meeting with Beirly.

"Huh?" I said. That's the kind of brilliant response I come up with when I'm talking to girls. Especially cute girls. And she was cute, with this wild, curly red hair.

The girl reached across me and grabbed the last cheeseburger. "That's how every first conversation starts here—what are you in for?"

At least she'd told me how to start the conversation. That helped. Somewhat. "Okay, uh, what are you in for?"

"If I tell you, you're not going to want to talk to me anymore," she answered.

I took a regular hamburger. Now what was I supposed to do? She was the one who told me to ask.

"Okay, I'll tell you," she went on. "First I let my fingernails grow really, really long. Then you know those three little bones that are right past the eardrum?"

"The malleus, the incus, and the stapes," I answered automatically. I grabbed a soda.

"I could tell you were smart." The girl smiled and moved a little closer. She had a strange odor. Sweet, like candy, but with an undertone of something pungent. I took a cautious sniff. Fertilizer, maybe?

"Anyway, I invited my best friend, Janice—my ex-best friend—to sleep over," the girl continued. "Then when she was asleep, I took the fingernail of my left pinky and—" She made a stabbing, twisting motion with her little finger. "Got all three at once."

She turned around and headed toward a table. I stared after her. I wasn't sure if I was supposed to follow her or not. I wasn't sure if I wanted to.

A tall guy with floppy black hair stopped next to me. "Maggie just told you the story about the fingernail and the little ear bones, didn't she?" He grinned. "And people say I have a sick sense of humor."

"That's not why she's in here?" I asked.

"She's not in here at all," the guy answered. "She's the kid of one of the doctors who works here. Dr. Nosek."

"Lot of doctors for a detention center," I commented. We headed over to the table where Maggie was sitting.

"Yeah," the guy said. "Psychiatrists, mostly. They want to rehabilitate us or something. I'm still trying to convince them I enjoy being twisted."

"You told him, didn't you, Danny?" Maggie demanded as soon as we sat down. "I can see it on his face."

"I forgot I crossed my heart and promised it would be our secret," Danny said sarcastically.

"Well, I'm not going to let anyone else have any fun either." Maggie stuck her tongue out at Danny. "He's in for assault. Fists, not fingernails, but the other guy was in the hospital for a week." She pointed to a guy in a T-shirt that said OBEY GRAVITY. IT'S THE LAW on the front. "That's Harlan Randazzo. He's been here a year for playing a prank at a Huskies football game."

"Actually, every Huskies football game since my brother made the team. I only got caught once," Harlan said. "I was going to have this giant doughnut rise out of the center yard line at halftime. I made it out of a weather balloon. But the timing got messed up. And there was a flammability issue. The field ended up taking a major hit, and the game had to be forfeited. At least none of my crew got nabbed. Only me."

"I still don't get why you did that," said Danny. "Even if it had gone off perfectly, what would you get out of it?"

"The pleasure of watching my perfect plan unfold. Of knowing I figured out how to make something work," Harlan explained.

"I get that," I said. And I did. Not the illegal part. But coming up with an intricate, clever plan and pulling it off . . . that was one of the cool parts of being an ATAC agent.

"Robert's the one I don't get," Maggie said. "He's in for streaking. And look at him. His body's not even that great."

"Hey," the thin boy sitting across from me— Robert—protested. He flexed his arm. A small muscle appeared. "I have plenty to show off. Besides, that's not why I was doing it. With everything that's going on in the world, we need a little fun. What's more fun than streaking? It's a completely goofy thing to do. Or see somebody do."

Joe hurried over and sat down with a tray of food. He looked a little stressed. I figured Dr. Beirly's blast of questions was the cause.

"This is my brother, Joe," I told the group.

"Please tell me the two of you are in here for something normal," Danny said.

"They're here because—" Maggie covered her mouth. "Oops. I guess I should at least pretend I don't read everybody's files when my mom leaves me alone in her office."

I made a mental note that Maggie would be a very good source of information. And that she wasn't very trustworthy.

"We hacked into Auction House," Joe answered. "We were skimming off two cents from every purchase."

"We were bringing in about ten grand a day," I bragged. Bragging seemed appropriate.

"*Nice,*" said Danny.

"A little too nice," Joe told him. "If we'd taken a little less, we might never have gotten caught."

"Is it okay if I sit here?" a girl with long blond hair asked. I noticed she had dark smudges under her eyes. She didn't look like she'd been sleeping well.

"No assigned seats in the torture chamber," Harlan told her.

"Come on. It's not that bad here," Robert protested. He turned to the blond girl. "We have movies every couple of nights. And field trips every weekend. Last weekend Elton—that's Dr. Beirly—and Micah took a bunch of us bungee jumping. People who didn't want to do that went to the mall with Maggie's mom. That's Maggie." Robert pointed her out and did the rest of the intros. The girl said her name was Lara Renner.

Harlan shook his head at Robert. "You get bought off pretty easy. A few movies and a ride on a big bouncy cord and you roll over? I hate this place. It's like the doctors here want to crack open our brains and rewire them. You know what? I'm happy with how I'm wired. I want my brain the way it is."

"I still say—," Robert began.

Harlan cut him off. "Talk to me when you've been here a year, like I have. This place needs a few flaming doughnuts to be dropped on it. Shut it down, that's what I say."

"Clearly this is the only detention center you've ever been in," Danny told him. "You wouldn't have lasted a week the place I was at before this, forget about a year."

A year. The first death, Gregory Teeter's, was about a year ago. Could Harlan be the killer? The pranks he pulled at those Huskies games sounded complex. He might have the chops to pull off a "haunting."

Name: Harlan Randazzo

Hometown: Newtown, CT

Physical description: 5'7", approximately 170 lbs., age 16, sandy hair, green eyes.

Occupation: Student/sentenced to the Undercliff House of Detention.

Background: Youngest of three brothers, skipped a grade in elementary school.

Suspicious behavior: Sentenced to Undercliff for playing an elaborate prank that took the kind of planning and cleverness creating a "ghost" would.

Suspected of: Murders of Maryama Soll and Gregory Teeter.

Possible motives: Hates the center and wants to close it down.

Lara tucked her hair behind her ears. "Has anyone . . . Do any of you have trouble sleeping here?"

"I don't think anyone sleeps very well the first few nights," said Robert. "It gets easier. There are a lot worse places you could have been sentenced to stay."

Danny laughed. "Like you'd know, streaker. You're so hard-core."

Robert blushed a little.

"I mean . . . never mind," Lara said.

Danny rolled his eyes. "It's the ghost thing again. You've already heard about the ghosts and you couldn't sleep."

"This place is supposed to be haunted?" asked Lara. "That's explains it, then. I'm really sensitive to spirits."

"Oh, come on," Danny groaned.

"There've been a lot of—," Maggie began. She stopped when a woman tapped her on the shoulder. "I'm done with my chemistry homework, Mom," Maggie told her.

So the woman was Dr. Nosek.

"That's great," Dr. Nosek told Maggie. "But you know that this part of the building is off-limits for you. Come on back to my office." Maggie reluctantly stood up and followed her mother away from the table.

"Tight leash," Joe commented when they were out of earshot.

"Yeah, our little Maggie got in some trouble over the summer," said Danny. "No one knows exactly what she did. But ever since then, she's been here every day after school and on weekends. She's supposed to be studying in her mother's office, but she's always wandering around."

"She makes her mom crazy. I heard Dr. Nosek lecturing her about how smart she is and how much potential she has. She's been winning these science awards practically since birth," Harlan added. "I love it. Her mother is trying to fix all of us, and her own daughter is about a step away from being in here for real."

"Do you mind telling me about the ghost?" Lara asked. "It would help if I knew more what I was dealing with. Last night a spirit kept trying to get a message through to me, but I couldn't understand."

"I wouldn't mind hearing either," Joe put in.

"Okay," said Harlan. "The thing is, this place used to be an insane asylum, starting back in the seventeen hundreds. One of the patients who died in the asylum is haunting Undercliff."

"Okay," Danny said. "The thing is, the people who believe that are brain damaged."

"I believe in the possibility that ghosts exist." Joe shot me a no-matter-what-you-say look.

"Forget possibility. I've seen one. In the room where they show the movies," Robert told us. "I left my jacket in there once, and when I went back to get it, I saw a man dressed in ragged old long johns. He was bleeding from the sides of his head and his arms. There were leeches on him. Big, fat ones. And he was screaming. Well, his mouth was open like he was screaming, but no sound was coming out. I ran up to him—"

"You ran up to him?" Joe broke in.

"Yeah. 'Cause he was bleeding. I wasn't thinking he was a ghost, even with the no-sound screaming. All I was thinking was, that dude is bleeding," Robert continued. "But right before I reached him, he disappeared."

"That's because he was never there." Danny said each word slowly, like that's what it would take to make Robert understand.

"I had something happen to me, too," Harlan revealed. "One night I had to sleep in the infirmary. And I was lying there in bed, and I swear, I felt these restraints wrap around me. Like they used to use on lunatics. I couldn't move my arms or my legs. I couldn't sit up. It was the scariest thing that's ever happened to me. I called my parents the next day and begged them to get me out of this place, but they said the court had put me here and I had to stay."

"You said you were in the infirmary, right?" I asked.

"Yeah," Harlan answered.

"Did you have a fever or anything?"

"Finally, someone sane!" Danny burst out. "Of course you had a fever. You had the flu. I remember. The whole thing was just some fever hallucination."

"It wasn't a hallucination. I can tell the difference," Harlan insisted. "And anyway, I found something behind the baseboard near the bed. There was this little hole dug into the stone, and I found this note in it." He pulled out a small piece of paper from his pocket.

"And you carry it around with you?" Danny asked.

"There's no safe place to keep anything here. You know that." Harlan placed the note in the center of the table so everyone could read it.

I felt a prickling sensation on the back of my neck. The handwriting was the same as the diary entry found with Maryama Soll's body. I quickly began to read.

Monday, April 30, 1810
My name is Moses Bottelle and I will not scream.
My name is Moses Bottelle and I will not scream.

I wont become one of them. I will stay sane. I will not scream.

Yet I feel that my doctor wants to hear me scream. He does not believe I am sane. That is too much to hope for, I suppose. Still, he pokes and prods me, as if he is hoping to uncover some darkness. Today he asked if I heard voices in my head, and he seemed disappointed when I told him I heard no imaginary people speaking to me. Why would that disappoint him?

I must think on my happy memories, although they are starting to grow dull with overuse. My nest and bird. My dinner and chess. My dogs. My sunrise. My turnips. I must cling to these. I will leave this place one day. I will stay sane until that day. I will not scream.

"Good job," Danny told Harlan a few minutes later, when we'd all had a chance to read the entry.

"What?" Harlan asked.

"What," Danny repeated, mocking him. "I mean, anyone who can make a big doughnut can write a few sentences that sound old-fashioned."

"I didn't write this," said Harlan. "Obviously, I could have. I have the skills. But I didn't."

"I believe you," Lara told him. "I know I was being contacted by a spirit last night. Maybe it was the spirit of Moses Bottelle. All I know for sure is that the spirit is going to stay trapped here at Undercliff unless we can figure out what it wants and how to help it."

"Right. And how exactly are we supposed to do that?" Danny asked.

"Simple," answered Lara. "We have a séance."

Killer Ghost

"A couple of announcements," Micah called from the front of the room as we were finishing up lunch. For tonight's entertainment, we've got two options at eight o'clock. We'll be showing *Puzzlecarver II* in the common room, or you can bake cookies in the kitchen."

"*Puzzlecarver II*. Cool. That's the one where the guy gets his intestines—," Robert began.

"Stop," Lara ordered.

"Too gross for you, princess?" asked Danny.

"No. I just haven't seen it," Lara told him, shoving her blond hair away from her face.

"And remember that next Saturday—yes, one week from today—is the test to qualify for the Winston

Beirly scholarship," Micah continued. "The test will cover all areas of science—biology, chemistry, physics, and whatever I'm leaving out. All the official stuff is on the bulletin board by the main entrance. Anyone can take the test—although I know some of you have been studying for almost a year. Highest score gets the scholarship—which will pay for four years of whatever college you can get yourself into."

"Winston Beirly. The man who won the Nobel Prize for his work in neurobiology?" I asked.

"Yep. He's our Beirly's father," Harlan said. "I guess Elton got his brains from the shallow end of the gene pool."

"He didn't seem that stupid at my intake interview. Although some of the questions were kinda weird," I commented. I looked over at Frank. He gave a quick nod. Clearly he'd gotten some whacked-out questions too.

"Come on. On one side you've got being the director of the Undercliff House of Detention. On the other side you've got winning the Nobel Prize," Harlan protested.

"Sounds like Daddy's a little smarter to me," agreed Danny. "Maybe we should discuss that at our next group therapy session with Dr. B. Maybe we should ask him how it *feels* to have a father who is so much more successful, and rich, and smart."

"And Nobel Prize–having," Harlan added. "I'm up for it. I'd love to see Beirly's face if we brought up his dad."

"Maybe he just feels proud," Robert suggested.

"Yeah, my dad just had this big art show in Manhattan, and I was totally proud of him," Lara added.

"But you're not almost forty and drawing greeting cards for a living. If you were, then you'd know how Beirly feels," Danny told her.

"My dad doesn't draw. He's more of a multimedia artist," said Lara.

"Now your after-lunch assignments," Micah announced. "Tables one and two: KP with Mrs. Hanson in the kitchen. Three and four: yard work with me. Tables five and six . . ."

"Four. That's us," Robert said. He grabbed his food tray and stood up. We all followed him over to the busing area, where we dumped our trash and left our trays and silverware to be washed.

"Yard people, follow me!" Micah called a few moments later. He led the way outside to a large shed. "Everybody grab a rake and some trash bags. Then take a section of lawn."

Frank and I liked to split up in situations like this. That way we could gather more info on more people in the shortest amount of time. I decided to work with Lara and Robert.

"So you think that's the deal with all ghosts?" I asked Lara as we started to rake. "You think they all just need some kind of help?"

"Yeah," said Robert. "There was this abandoned construction site near my house that was supposed to be haunted. Supposedly, if you went in there, you'd feel these hands wrap around your throat. If you didn't get out fast enough, you'd suffocate. That doesn't sound like a cry for help to me."

"It's not always easy for a spirit to communicate. Maybe the spirit was trying to explain that it had been strangled," Lara suggested. "Maybe it wanted help tracking down its killer."

"It just doesn't make sense." Robert started scooping a pile of leaves into one of the trash bags.

Lara shook her head. "Does it make sense to you that a spirit would want to hang around for years just to scare people? When it could move on to the next plane of existence?"

"Not really," Robert admitted.

"I can think of a few people who might be sick enough to find it entertaining, but not many," I agreed.

"Why would that guy Moses want to stay at Undercliff at all?" Robert asked. "If he is the ghost. Wouldn't he want to stay in a place where he was happier?"

"You're not getting it," said Lara. "Most of the spirits who stay attached to our world don't really have a choice. Some of them don't even know they're dead. But a lot of them have something they need to finish before they move on."

"Like what?" I asked.

Lara's blue eyes darkened. "Like if someone's hurt them and nobody knows. A spirit might not be at peace until the truth is exposed and the person is punished." Her voice was tight with anger. She was really serious about this stuff.

"Okay, so say Moses wants revenge and I wanted to help—which I might not, because I'm a non-violent kind of guy—who would I be getting revenge on?" Robert asked. "All the doctors who worked at the asylum are already dead. Everybody he knew is dead."

"I wasn't saying that Moses—or any spirit—is looking for a human to go out and physically hurt someone. But maybe Moses would want the truth about the treatment the patients received at the asylum to come out in a magazine article. Or maybe he wants his descendants tracked down and told something."

"I'd definitely be up for bringing out the truth about Undercliff back when it was an asylum, if that's what Moses wants," said Robert. "Beirly brought in a psychic about a month ago. You don't want to hear what she picked up from some of the rooms." He shook his head. "Gruesome. Extremely gruesome."

"There was a psychic at Undercliff?" Lara exclaimed. "Why? What happened?"

Robert stopped raking. "What really made him do it was that somebody died. No, actually, two people died. Two kids. And then there was a girl who killed herself after that. I wasn't here when the first guy died. But I was when Maryama died about two months ago. And everybody started saying the ghost killed her and the first guy, too. Beirly said he brought the psychic in to do a cleansing because the patients in the asylum had been mistreated. But I think he was really just trying to calm people down."

"Wait. A ghost is supposed to have killed two kids in this place?" I asked. I needed to hear any gossip there was to hear about the deaths.

"Yeah," Robert answered. "I thought about streaking during dinner one night about a week after Maryama died, just to lighten things up. But even watching some idiot run around naked wasn't going to make anybody feel better."

"And everyone really believes the ghost killed her? Them, I mean? Or is it just a spooky story people like to tell?" asked Lara. It was exactly what I wanted to know.

"Everyone was scared. I know that for sure," Robert answered. "Some people acted like they didn't believe. But I think everyone did, at least a little. And the psychic doing the cleansing got things sort of back to normal, even though she freaked everybody out, too."

"What do you mean?" I asked.

"She went into every room and cracked a window. Then she waved some burning sage around and told any spirits there to go toward the light. That part was okay," Robert explained. "But in some rooms, it was almost like she'd go into a trance. She'd start talking about what had happened right where she was standing." Robert stared off into space. It was almost like *he'd* gone into a trance for a minute.

"Less talking, more raking," Micah called as he walked by carrying an armload of clothes. "I'm just going to the parking lot. Be right back."

Lara, Robert, and I quickly returned to work.

"Hey, Micah," a kid shouted from the main entrance. "Elton said he forgot to tell you to tell the cleaners there's a stain on the front of the gray suit jacket."

Micah turned and waved. "Got it."

"So what kinds of things did the psychic say?" I asked when Micah was out of earshot.

Robert kept raking as he answered. "In one room—it was the girl's dorm—she said she was spinning and spinning and spinning. Then she screamed, because she felt blood coming out of her ear."

"There was real blood—or she just felt it in her trance?" Lara asked nervously.

"There were a few drops of real blood," Robert told her. "Beirly said that she was probably experiencing an old treatment for mental illness. I guess doctors used to think that if you were mentally ill, your blood was congested in your brain. Spinning you around and around really fast in a hanging chair was supposed to help cure you by thinning out any blood clots."

"That's so horrible," Lara cried.

"You know what's really horrible?" Robert stopped raking again. "Before the psychic ever said anything, kids had felt dizzy in that room, like they were spinning around and around and around. And they felt cold up in the waiting room outside Beirly's office, even before she did her trance thing up there and started shivering."

The waiting room. Where I'd felt the cold spot.

"What did she say happened in the waiting room?" I asked.

"The doctors had different kinds of water therapy they used on the patients—that's how Beirly explained what she was feeling. Sometimes they put a patient into a tub of ice and made them stay there for hours and hours. Beirly said patients even died if the doctors timed it wrong," Robert answered.

Tub of ice. Ice cubes. *Click-click-clack.*

A shiver ripped through me. If Micah hadn't gotten me out of the waiting room this morning, how long would I have sat there?

Hours and hours?

Until I froze to death?

You Know I Did It

"**H**ere's one for you," Harlan said. He used both hands to scoop leaves into a trash bag. "If you're holding a Slinky at the top and then let it drop, which way does the bottom of the Slinky move initially?"

Down seemed like the obvious answer. But the spring had been uncoiled before it was released. That could mean it would recoil and the bottom would—

"Doesn't go either way," Danny said before I could finish going through the logic of the physics problem. "The bottom of the spring doesn't know the top has been released when it's first dropped."

"Oh, right!" I got it. "The information wave has

to travel through the Slinky before the bottom of it is affected at all."

Danny and Harlan both stopped working for a moment and looked at me. "So are you going to be taking the test for the scholarship?"

"The one Dr. Beirly's dad is giving out?" I shrugged. "I hadn't thought about it yet. You think I should?"

Now Danny and Harlan looked at each other. "If you're up for the humiliation," Danny answered. "A bunch of us have been studying since the thing was announced about a year ago."

"It's pretty much down to the two of us," Harlan added. "Now that Maryama—" He stopped short.

This was something I definitely needed to know more about. "Who's Maryama?" I asked. I wanted to learn everything I could about the girl whose death Joe and I were here to investigate.

"She was this girl who was studying with us for the test," Danny muttered. "She died a while ago."

"Man." I shook my head. "How'd that happen?"

"Danny found her," said Harlan. "Ask him."

"We came up with some practice chemistry problems for each other," Danny began. "I was bringing mine over to the girls' dorm. There was some movie everyone wanted to see downstairs, so she was all alone."

Danny started raking harder, digging the metal teeth into a patch of ground that was already leaf free. He didn't say anything for so long, I wondered if he was going to tell me the rest of what happened. Finally he started talking again.

"She was lying on the floor near the door. Like maybe she'd been trying to crawl out. There was a little blood coming out of her nose. And a little coming out of one ear. And her mouth—it was all twisted, like she'd been about to scream." Danny threw down the rake. "That enough information for you?" He stalked away before I could answer.

"He's just . . . he got questioned a lot, because he found Maryama's body," Harlan told me. "I guess I shouldn't have made him talk about it. But he's the only one who knows anything. Beirly got her body out of the building ASAP, and he made this announcement about how sad he and everyone at Undercliff was about her dying. That was it. Until all these rumors started about the ghost offing her."

"Do people really believe that?" I asked.

"After what happened to me in the infirmary, I can believe anything," Harlan answered. "I swear I couldn't move that night. I couldn't see any restraints, but they were on me. If a ghost could do that, why couldn't it kill somebody?"

Danny reappeared and dumped a bunch of trash

bags in front of us—even though we still had a ton.

"That must have been really hard, finding the body," I said.

"Whatever." Danny turned to Harlan. "Hey, less competition for the scholarship, right?"

Harlan gave a forced laugh. "Yeah. And it's a good thing for us kids of the staff can't enter. Maggie would pound us."

"You, maybe," Danny said. "I could take her. That scholarship is mine. I'm getting that money, leaving home, going to college, and never looking back."

That's hard-core, I thought. *He really wants to win.*

Had Danny been afraid Maryama would do better on the test and snatch the scholarship away from him? He was at Undercliff because he'd assaulted someone. So he had the potential for violence. But that didn't mean he killed her. Did it?

SUSPECT PROFILE

Name: Danny Laybourn

Hometown: Fairfield, Connecticut

Physical description: 5'11", approximately 180 lbs., age 17, black hair, brown eyes.

Occupation: Student/sentenced to the Undercliff House of Detention.

I carefully squeezed the toothpaste out onto my brush, making sure to roll the tube up as I went. I'm always pretty neat with the paste—unlike Joe, who sometimes even manages to get some in his hair—but tonight I was going extra slow. I wanted to be the last one done so Joe and I could have the bathroom to ourselves. We needed to update each other. We hadn't had any time alone since we came into Undercliff this morning.

Joe was following my lead, giving his teeth the most meticulous brushing they'd ever had. Our dentist would thank me. "Find out anything good?" I asked once the bathroom had emptied out.

"Big Boy trash bags are a lot stronger than Mighty Mower," he answered.

"Ha, Ha, ha," I said.

Joe rolled his eyes. "I found out a lot more stuff about the ghost," he told me. "Lara thinks maybe Moses is haunting Undercliff because he wants revenge on the doctors who used those hideous treatments on him and the other patients. Or maybe he just wants people to know what went on here. She's definitely going to try to find out exactly what he wants tonight at the séance."

"I was thinking more of evidence or motives for suspects," I told him. "We can't run this investigation with the theory that a ghost is behind Maryama and Gregory's deaths," I told him.

"You can't prove that ghosts don't exist," Joe protested.

I shoved my hands through my hair. I wasn't going to win this one. Especially not in the few minutes we had to talk. "Look, can we at least agree to put the ghost at the bottom of our suspect list?" I asked. "I have some ideas why it's more likely that Danny or Harlan is our killer."

"Okay, tell," said Joe.

"Well, Harlan hates this place. He'd love to shut it down. Creating a ghost that was killing kids would be a good way to do it," I explained. "And those pranks he pulls . . ."

"Show he has the skills to pull off some creepy

haunting effects," Joe finished for me.

"Right. And get this. It turns out Danny is a complete science head, too. It seems like he and Harlan are both front-runners to win that scholarship," I continued.

"So Danny might have the chops to come up with some ghost special effects too," said Joe. "But what would his motive be? He doesn't seem to think Undercliff is all that bad. From what he said at lunch, it sounded like he'd been in worse places."

"The motive is that Maryama was the big competition for the scholarship," I said. "We need to find out if Gregory was going for the scholarship too. Maybe Danny killed them both to make sure he gets the highest score on that test."

"Bed check in five," I heard Micah call from down the hall.

"We better get back in there," I said.

"About the ghost thing," Joe began. "I'm not going to try to convince you the ghost should be our number-one suspect. But I still think this place could be haunted for real, Frank. When I was in Beirly's waiting room, I ended up in a cold spot. I could see my breath and everything. If Micah hadn't realized I was starting to go hypothermic . . ." He shook his head.

"I don't know what would have happened."

Joe was completely serious. He wasn't trying to mess with my head.

"There are several nonparanormal reasons for one section of a room to be colder than another," I began.

"I'm not talking a few degrees colder," Joe burst out. "Were you listening? I could see my breath."

"It's October in Connecticut," I reminded him. "It's cold out. And there are some psychological factors. You came into this place expecting it to be haunted. You watched all those *Spectral* episodes—and one of them even talked about cold spots. You—"

"So you think all my ATAC training just disappeared? You think I couldn't tell reality from my own imagination?" Joe demanded, his voice rising.

"Keep it down," I told him. "I think it's normal to have some psychological reaction to a place like this. That was even in our training, remember?"

Joe gave a curt nod.

"I also think it's very likely that someone has been creating hauntings in the building. What you experienced could have been set up in advance," I said.

"Later I found out that room was where patients

got ice baths," Joe pointed out. "And when I was in the cold spot, I heard sounds like ice cubes knocking into each other."

"I heard the room was used for that too. Beirly told me," I said. "Probably everyone who has been here for a few days has heard that story."

"Beirly talked about the hauntings?" Joe asked.

"Yeah. I thought it was kind of weird for him to bring it up to a new guy," I answered.

"I thought he was kind of weird, period," said Joe. "Those questions weren't like any of the psych tests we had to take before we became field agents." ATAC makes kids go through some pretty intensive physical and psychological evaluations— plus a ton of training—before they are allowed on missions.

"Definitely not," I agreed. "He even told me he brought in a psychic to cleanse the building in case there were spirits."

"I heard about that too," said Joe.

"So it's not like the ghost is something a few kids whisper about," I commented.

"I guess if I was going to do a fake haunting here, I'd use stuff everybody's heard about the badness that went on at Undercliff when it was an asylum. It would just make the whole thing sound more real." He looked me in the eye. "But I'm still not sure what happened to me today was faked."

"We've only been here a day," I reminded him. "I'm not sure about anything. Except that we better get into the dorm before bed check."

"Yeah," Joe said. "Lara's going to come get us for the séance at about eleven thirty. She wants to start at midnight."

"Okay." I followed him back into the dorm. I managed to make it into bed about half a minute before Micah came in to do a head count. The guy definitely worked a long day.

I knew it would be a good idea to get some sleep before the séance. But my brain was too busy processing everything that I'd already observed at Undercliff. My thoughts jerked among the three suspects we had so far: Beirly, Harlan, and Danny.

Well, and the ghost, if I wanted to keep a completely open mind. But that was a theory I just didn't buy.

Danny didn't believe in the ghost either. I wondered what he thought had happened to Maryama. Assuming that he didn't kill her himself. The scholarship offered him a huge amount of freedom. A second chance. It could change his life.

The scholarship was a motive for Harlan, too. Or maybe he was angry enough to want to shut the place down for no other reason than how much he hated it. For a guy like him—a guy whose idea of fun was breaking the rules—living here had to be extra hard. Even though Danny was right about Undercliff being an easier detention center than other places. Joe and I had gone undercover at a juvie center out in the woods that would have made Harlan's head turn inside out. Orders were shouted at you pretty much every second, every day at that place.

Beirly seemed to want kids to have some fun while they were here. Maybe he blurted out everything about the ghost and the psychic and all that because he thought it was the way to build trust. Maybe he thought if he was up-front with the kids who came to Undercliff, then they'd be up-front with him.

My head started to feel heavy. I was on information overload. I'd go over all this with Joe tomorrow. . . .

"Hey, Frank," someone said softly. I opened my eyes and saw Danny standing over me. "You know I did it, don't you?" He gave my bed a kick, and it spun like it was on casters.

Danny jammed his foot down on the mattress to stop the spin. "You know I killed Maryama. And Gregory, too." He grinned at me. "Want to know something else? I enjoyed it. I was trying to kill that guy I put in the hospital."

I tried to sit up, but he gave the bed another kick. And it whirled. Out of the corner of my eye, I could see the other beds going past in a blur. Joe was asleep. Everyone was asleep.

Finally the bed slowed to a stop. I felt like my brain was rotating in my skull. I blinked hard to clear my vision and saw Harlan standing next to Danny. "That was nothing," Harlan said. "Want to see a real prank?"

He jerked my bed upright with one hand, then spun it. It was like being on the Gravitron at the school carnival. I should have fallen off the bed, but I was pinned to it by g-force.

Bang! The bed slammed to the floor. Beirly had joined Danny and Harlan. "Good work," he told them. "That should have thinned out the nasty clots in his brain."

I let out a thin moan. Then it hit me. I was dreaming.

Wake up, I told myself. *All you have to do is* wake up.

I forced my eyes open and sat up. I did a quick scan of the room. Danny and Harlan were both asleep in their beds. Beirly was nowhere around.

Of course not, I thought. *Because you were dreaming.*

Except . . .

Except that the moaning sound I'd been making in the dream—I could still hear it. It wasn't coming from me. It was coming from out in the hall. Low and soft.

And I was wide awake.

The Séance

*O*oooh. *Ooooh*. The moaning sound jerked me awake. My heart pounded in my throat. I don't know how it got up there, but that's where it was.

Then it hit me. The *ooooh*ing. It had to be Lara signaling that it was time to meet up for the séance. I checked my watch. Yep, eleven thirty.

I looked over at Frank. He had his "I'm trying very hard to find the logic" face on. "Séance time," I mouthed to him.

He nodded, like he had known that the whole time. But he so hadn't.

I climbed out of bed, put on my sneakers, and pulled a jacket on over my pajamas. Then I crept across the dark dorm and out the door. Lara and a girl with short brown hair were waiting in the hall. A few moments later Frank, Danny, Harlan, and Robert joined us.

"You brought Cyndi?" Danny asked, shooting an angry look at the short-haired girl. "She's one of Beirly's little pets."

"Cyndi's one of the kids who's been here the longest. I thought she might come up with a connection to something we get during the séance. Ghosts don't always communicate in a way that's clear to the living," Lara said. She adjusted one of her pink bunny slippers. It was about to slide off her foot.

"Beirly better not hear about this," Danny told Cyndi. "Or I'll know exactly who to come looking for."

That sounded pretty much like a threat. And a threat wasn't what you wanted to hear from someone who was in a detention center for assault. Cyndi didn't look too worried, though.

"Let's go," said Harlan. "No one's going to have to tell Beirly if we keep standing out here talking. Where are we going, anyway? Not that I don't like surprises."

"Cyndi said there's a chapel. That's where I want to do it," Lara told him.

"Let's go down the back stairs," Danny suggested.

"Beirly works late a lot, and if we go the other way, we have to walk practically right outside his office."

"That staircase is always locked," Robert reminded him.

"Not a problem." Danny took the lead, and we followed him to a narrow door at the end of the hall. It was locked. Danny pulled an unwound paper clip out of his pocket, slid it into the lock, twisted a few times, and the door opened. It was like he had some ATAC training or something.

Nobody had bothered to paint the back stairway in let's-all-be-happy colors. It was the same dull gray as the outside of the building. Our footsteps echoed as we headed down the granite stairs.

"We should have the séance right here," Cyndi said. "This seems to me like a place a ghost would hang out."

It's kind of what I was thinking.

We came out of the stairway into the kitchen pantry. "Why aren't we trying to contact Moses in one of the places we know he's been?" Robert asked as we headed through the kitchen and out into the dining hall. "Like the infirmary. I'm pretty sure no one's sick. It should be empty."

"Lara was saying before that she didn't want a place where there are bad memories for Moses," Robert told him.

"And from what I've heard, every spot he's appeared is also a place where it's very likely he experienced a lot of physical and mental pain," said Lara. "We want to communicate in a place that feels safe to him."

"I thought ghosts didn't like churches," Harlan commented.

"That's vampires," Lara said.

"That, and demon spawn," I added.

"You guys don't believe in those, too, do you?" Danny asked. He stuck his head out into the hall and did a quick check. "All clear."

"If you don't believe in ghosts, why are you even here?" Lara snapped.

"There aren't any other activities scheduled right now. I should put a note about that in the suggestion box—need more events for insomniacs," Danny answered. "Come on." He trotted down the hall to the right, then ducked inside the chapel. The rest of us were right behind him.

The only light came from the half moon shining through the circular stained-glass window at the front of the room. Robert started for the light switch. "No!" Lara grabbed him by the sleeve, stopping him. "No electricity. It can interfere with the communication."

"We brought candles," Cyndi said.

"How'd you get candles?" asked Robert.

"There are a bunch in the top shelf of the supply closet. In case the power goes out," Cyndi replied.

"See? It's good to have an old-timer around," Lara pointed out. "Let's sit in a circle in front of the pews."

"Or hey, we could sit on the pews, since that's what they're designed for," Harlan suggested.

"A circle is an important part of a séance," Lara told him. "Sit down, everyone."

Once we were all on the floor, Lara pulled candles out of this knapsack purse kind of thing she had over her shoulder. "I'm going to pass the candles around. We all need to hold them for a moment and envision peaceful smoke coming out of them. This is called charging the candles."

Danny snickered. Lara glared at him. "The attitude of the participants is really important. If you're going to treat this like a big joke, then we need you to leave. We're trying to help the spirit trapped here at Undercliff find rest, okay?"

"Okay," said Danny. Lara handed him one of the candles, and he closed his eyes and at least gave the impression that he was doing the charging thing. When I got a candle, I did my best to picture peaceful smoke coming out of the top—even though I really wasn't sure how peaceful smoke looked that much different from regular smoke. Fluffier, maybe? Swirlier?

Once all the candles had been passed around the group, Lara set them up in the center of the circle and lit them. She opened a little paper package filled with brown powder and set it in front of her.

"What's that?" Robert asked.

"Cinnamon. The scent is supposed to provide warmth and energy. It's welcoming for spirits," explained Lara. "We should be using incense, but I didn't have any."

"I can't smell it at all," Danny said.

"We'll have to hope spirits are more sensitive than you," Lara told him. "Shouldn't be hard."

"I'm wounded. I'm wounded because I'm deeply sensitive," Danny protested.

I snorted. Lara frowned at me. "Sorry," I said. But I couldn't help it. That was pretty funny.

"All right. Let's get started. There are a couple of things you need to know," Lara said. "If we do get a spirit to appear, nobody scream or make any loud sounds. And don't all start asking questions at once. I'll ask the questions. It will be less confusing."

"What if Moses doesn't want to have a chat?" asked Robert. "What if he wants to show us how it felt to be in restraints or something?"

Or how it felt to be in an ice bath, I couldn't help thinking.

"We break the circle. We'll be holding hands, and that means we let go. Then I'll blow out the candles and ask Moses to leave in peace. Frank, you're closest to the light switch. You turn on the lights if things go bad," Lara instructed.

Frank nodded.

"Let's begin. Everyone join hands," Lara said.

I took Harlan's hand in my right and Lara's in my left. Lara's hand was damp with sweat. She'd sounded totally calm when she'd been giving us the rundown on the séance, but she was nervous.

Harlan's hand was dry, but he was holding my hand kind of tight. I figured that meant he was nervous too. I'll admit that I was. I wondered if any little part of Frank was starting to believe ghosts might exist.

"Take some deep breaths," said Lara, her voice lower now, softer. "In through your nose and out through your mouth. Watch the candles and breathe. Let your minds go blank. Open yourselves to the world beyond this one."

The blank mind thing is hard. Try it and see. First I started thinking that I could be holding hands with a killer. I shoved that out of my head. Then I started thinking that I might see an actual ghost in, like, a minute. I pushed that out of my head too. *Then* I started thinking that Monkey Madness ice cream would be even better if it had banana chips in it too, because they are so crunchy. I like crunchy stuff in my ice cream. Chewy stuff, too. Frank likes his ice cream with nothing in it but ice cream. He's pretty boring—

"Someone in the circle isn't open to the world beyond. Watch the candles and breathe," Lara coached.

Right. I picked one of the candle flames and stared at it, concentrating on each tiny flicker.

"Our beloved Moses, we ask that you commune with us and move among us," Lara finally said. "Everyone now."

"Our beloved Moses, we ask that you commune with us and move among us," we all repeated with her. "Our beloved Moses, we ask that you commune with us and move among us. Our beloved Moses, we ask that you commune with us and move among us."

Each time we spoke the words, I felt like someone was giving my guts a twist. And we kept on chanting. "Our beloved Moses, we ask that you commune with us and move among us."

At last Lara raised her voice and cried out, "If you are among us, Moses, please reveal yourself!"

The room went silent. I didn't even hear anyone breathing. I know I wasn't. I was waiting to see what Moses was going to do. I scanned the faces in the circle. Robert looked freaked out. Frank looked like he was taking mental notes on everything. Lara had this intense, listening-hard expression on her face. Danny looked kind of bored. Harlan looked freaked out to a slightly lesser degree than Robert. And Cyndi . . . Cyndi's mouth was open. It was like she was screaming, but no sound was coming out.

"Cyndi, what's wrong?" I asked. I didn't say it loud. I remembered what Lara said about nobody screaming or making loud sounds.

Cyndi closed her mouth, swallowed hard, then opened it again and said, "Behind you."

Without breaking the circle, I turned my head. About halfway down the aisle that ran between the rows of pews, a mist was forming. Swirling. Growing thicker. Harlan's fingers tightened on my hand until I swear I could hear bones crunching.

"Moses, is that you?" Lara asked.

"No," a voice answered. High and squeaky. It didn't sound human.

"Can you tell us who you are?" Lara asked.

"I don't remember." It was kind of like listening to a rusty door hinge talking.

"Were you a patient at the Undercliff Asylum?" Lara continued.

"I don't remember."

"What do you remember?" asked Lara.

"Someone hurt me," the spirit squealed. "Someone hurt me," it repeated, and the sound of its voice changed, became lower, softer. Human. Female.

Across the circle from me, Danny's eyes went wide. I jerked my head back toward the mist. Something was moving in it now. Forming.

Blond hair. Pale face. A girl. About my age. A dress blowing around her legs. Her lips opened. "Somebody hurt me," she said.

And Cyndi screamed. The sound bounced off the walls of the chapel. "I know who it is!" she cried. "Get her away from me! Please, please. Keep her away from me!"

Think He Saw Us?

I figured this qualified as things going bad. I jumped up and flicked on the lights. "It's Iris!" Harlan exclaimed.

"Iris, are you okay? What do you need from us?" called Robert.

"I'm the only one who should talk to the spirit," Lara reminded us.

"Keep her away from me!" Cyndi screamed. "She's come back to get me!"

"We're closing the circle. Now." Lara blew out the candles.

"She's gone, Cyndi," Joe said. "You're okay. She's gone. See?"

I whipped my head toward the misty spot where

the girl had appeared, surrounded by shimmering light. There was only mist now. Mist that was beginning to fade away.

"What happened?" Robert asked. "I thought we were going to get Moses. That wasn't Moses."

"I need to finish closing the circle," said Lara, her voice rough and urgent. "What was her name? Anybody—what was her name?"

"Iris Edwards," Robert told her.

Cyndi wrapped her arms around herself. "I—I didn't know she hated me that much."

"Iris Edwards, go in peace! Iris Edwards, go in peace! Iris Edwards, go in peace!" Lara commanded. Then she held up her hands and made "quiet down" motions at all of us. She closed her eyes for a long moment. "I don't sense the presence anymore. Her spirit has left us."

"We should probably get out of here too," Joe suggested. "We've been making kind of a lot of noise."

"So what did you do to make that Iris chick hate you so much?" asked Danny. "Coming back from the grave. That's hard-core."

I definitely wanted to know the answer to that question. Not that I would have asked it that way. I wouldn't have asked it while Cyndi was still shivering with fear, either.

"She killed herself," Robert said. "Maybe that's why she came back. Aren't people who killed themselves supposed to be restless spirits?" he asked Lara.

"I didn't get the sense that she had taken her own life," Lara answered. "Is there any other reason she could have come back?"

"I never even talked to the girl when she was alive," Danny muttered.

"Maybe that's why she's back. She had a crush," Joe joked. I apologize for my brother. He doesn't always have an appropriate sense of humor.

"What about you, Cyndi?" asked Lara. "You seem to think Iris wanted to hurt you. Why?"

"It's none of your business," Cyndi snapped.

"I kind of think it's all our business," Harlan told her. "She might have accidentally sucked out our eyeballs when she was coming after you."

"Sucked out our eyeballs! How'd you come up with that?" Robert asked. "I've never heard of a ghost—"

"Be quiet for a minute," I told the group. "I think I hear somebody coming."

Yeah, there were definitely footsteps heading down the hall toward the chapel. "You know a back way out of here?" I asked Danny.

He shook his head. "The only doors open into the main hallway."

"I've got an idea," said Joe. "There's a window not very far down the hall. I'll go out it, and make a lot of noise doing it. Whoever's out there will go after me—by going out the front door, probably. That will give the rest of you time to bolt."

"Why would you—," Danny began.

"No time," said Joe.

He was right. The footsteps were really close now.

"I'm gone." Joe headed for the door. I followed him. I wasn't letting him go without backup.

We slipped into the hall, keeping low. But we were still spotted immediately.

"Hold up," a voice called out. I was pretty sure it was Micah.

Joe slid open the window. I guess the center depended on the high-tech security gate to keep all of us inside Undercliff, where we belonged. He slithered out. I was right behind him. So close I actually landed on him.

"Glad I could be your air bag," Joe muttered as he pushed himself to his feet. Then we were off. I didn't hear anyone behind us. Made sense. Most adults wouldn't take the window route.

"Think he saw us?" Joe asked as we ran.

"He definitely saw us, but I think just our backs," I answered.

"Front door?" Joe called as we neared it. It wasn't

a bad choice. We were trying to get Micah's attention. But if we could do that and not get caught, it would be better.

"Fire escape!" I burst out. "Around the corner." I'd seen it when we were doing the lawn work.

"Excellent!" said Joe.

We raced around the corner and skidded to a stop under the fire escape. I made my hands into a stirrup and boosted Joe into the air. He grabbed the bottom of the metal ladder and gave it a yank. Good thing we weren't trying to be quiet, because it clanged and clattered all the way to the ground.

We took the ladder up to the third floor. Overshooting the floor our dorm was on seemed like a smart idea. The window we climbed in led to a storeroom. We picked our way through a disorganized jumble of junk: some chairs like the ones in Beirly's waiting room that needed reupholstering, a couple of metal tanks—empty oxygen tanks, I figured—boxes filled with extension cords and old computer parts and other electronic junk.

"I think we've given the others time to get back from the chapel," I said to Joe.

He nodded. We slipped out into the hall and softly shut the door behind us. Now we needed to worry about getting ourselves back to the dorm without getting caught.

"Back stairs?" Joe whispered.

I answered by leading the way down to them. I pulled out my lock picks—I always carry them—and got the door open in about the same amount of time Danny had with a paper clip.

We slowly walked down the stairs. Slowly so our feet wouldn't make a sound. I opened the door that led to the second floor.

And a hand grabbed me by the arm.

JOE

Inside the Bag

I jerked Frank back into the stairwell. "Flashlight," I said softly.

He nodded.

I did a slow count in my head. *One Mississippi, two Mississippi, three Mississippi* . . . When I got to ten, I nudged Frank.

"A little longer," he whispered.

A little longer turned out to be about a million and four Mississippi. If you ever go on a stealth operation with my brother, make sure to hit the bathroom first.

Finally he eased open the door. We both peered into the hallway. No flashlight beam this time. I'd decided it was clear about thirteen Mississippis

89

before Frank did. How long does it really take to thoroughly examine a hallway for something the size of a person? I mean, seriously.

When we stepped out into the hall, I darted around Frank and took the lead. I knew he'd keep up with me even if he wanted to stop and do a full 360-degree scan every few feet. It's a big-brother thing. He thinks he has to protect me.

FRANK

Frank here. What I have to protect Joe from is doing something stupid.

JOE

Out. I'm telling this part.

So anyway, Frank followed me back to the dorm. I veered off to the bathroom. Frank followed me there, too.

"Who do you think staged the ghost appearance?" he asked before I could do what I'd gone in there to do.

"Are you absolutely sure it was staged? The way the mist appeared . . . and that girl . . . her voice. Remember how it sounded at first? It wasn't even like a human. And then when she said, 'Somebody hurt me,' it gave me the full-on wiggins," I told him.

"We're having mist in our UNICEF haunted house," Frank reminded me.

"Yeah. But we're using dry ice. There were no tubs of dry ice in the back of the chapel," I shot back.

"Some of the fog machines we priced were really small," he said. "There could have been one under a pew or something. And the voice—there are all kinds of ways to modify voices."

"Okay, fine, whatever," I told him. "What about the girl? She appeared out of nowhere. How could someone have done that?"

"It's been done. It's done every day at Disney World on that Haunted Mansion ride," Frank answered. "Or did you think those were real ghosts in there?"

Frank sometimes gets a little sarcastic when he's freaked out. "Come on, that's a Pepper's Ghost illusion," I said. "There's no way that's what was going on in the chapel tonight. Or are you really telling me you think there is a room with a mirror image of the chapel behind a sheet of glass? We would have had to walk right through it when we came into the room."

"I wasn't saying that the girl was in a mirror image room and that her image was being reflected into the main room," Frank protested. "All I was saying is that there are ways to create the illusion we saw. Pepper's Ghost is one way. And I bet a guy like Harlan Randazzo knows some others."

"Because he plays pranks?" I asked.

"And because he's really into science," Frank answered. "The Pepper's Ghost illusion depends on science and math. Pepper actually had a degree in chemistry."

"But Harlan didn't come up with the idea of the séance," I reminded Frank. "Lara did."

"True." Frank thought for a moment. "Lara suggested the séance at lunch, though. That gave Harlan hours to get things set up in the chapel."

"I guess if I was trying to make everyone think Undercliff was haunted, I definitely wouldn't want a séance to happen without a ghost making an appearance," I said.

Frank frowned. "Except . . . Lara didn't mention the chapel. So how would Harlan—or whoever our perp is—know to set up there?"

"She may have told someone when we weren't around," I said. "She wasn't keeping the details secret or anything." I shook my head. "I still don't get how the girl appeared."

"Let's forget about the how for a little while," Frank suggested. "Let's focus on the who."

A suspect rundown seemed like a smart idea.

"Okay, we've got Harlan. Smart, really smart, likes to play pranks, hates Undercliff, could be doing the hauntings to try to shut it down in a warped way."

"Hauntings and murders," said Frank.

"Right," I answered. "He was in the room when the ghost appeared. But I'm not sure we know everyone who was in the room. Somebody could have been hiding in there before we showed up."

"Good point. But for now, let's stay with the people we know for sure were there. Danny has the science to figure out how to pull off a complex illusion," Frank said.

"I understand how Maryama Soll's death helped him. It eliminated competition for the scholarship, and Danny really wanted to win it." I tapped my forehead. It's this thing I do when I'm thinking. "But what would pulling a ghost illusion at the séance do for him?"

"Well, it keeps up the idea that Undercliff is haunted," Frank answered. "That keeps attention away from him as a suspect in Maryama's murder."

"As long as there's a ghost around, there are going to be a lot of people who think the ghost is the one killing people," I agreed. "We need to find out more about Gregory Teeter. See if there's any motive for Danny wanting him dead."

"The only two other people we know for sure

were in the chapel are Cyndi and Robert," Frank said. "Besides us, of course."

I held up my hands. "Don't look at me. I do think you should have an open mind and consider the possibility that ghosts exist—and that maybe one exists right here at Undercliff. But I didn't stage one for you."

"And I didn't stage one for you just so I could later prove it was staged and finally convince you that ghosts *don't* exist," Frank stated.

"So Robert and Cyndi," I said.

"Robert and Cyndi," repeated Frank. "Nothing I've noticed about Robert has made me think of him as a possible suspect. At least not yet."

"Me either. And we know almost zero about Cyndi—except for seeing the way she lost it at the séance," I said. "What was that about?"

"That's something we definitely have to dig into," Frank told me. "We should get some sleep. We have a lot to do tomorrow."

"I just have one more question," I said. "About the ghost."

"How the illusion was created?"

"No. Why was the ghost that girl? If someone has been trying to make everybody believe Undercliff is haunted, why did they switch ghosts?" I asked. "Why not stick with Moses? All the other incidents have been connected to him or the insane asylum. Why go with this girl Iris?"

"I don't know," Frank admitted.

"Maybe that's something we need to start working on tomorrow too," I said.

The image of Iris's face filled my mind. Her lips moved, and I could almost hear her saying, "Somebody hurt me."

"That hurt," Cyndi muttered. I bet it did. Lara had given her a hard elbow to the ribs while she guarding Cyndi in a postbreakfast b-ball game. Chuck, the guy supervising us, didn't notice. I could see why. Lara was fast, and Chuck was on the opposite side of the court.

Cyndi twisted around Lara and pounded down the court. We both got ourselves as close to the basket as we could as Robert—our teammate—took a wild shot from outside the perimeter.

Didn't make it. Not even close. Didn't even hit the backboard.

Frank snagged the ball and started toward his team's basket. Lara got right on Cyndi. I guarded Danny. Frank did a nice behind-the-back pass to a girl with a long braid who'd managed to position herself almost under the basket. Nice for his team, I mean.

Whap! I heard the sound of a body hitting the wooden floor.

Skweet! Chuck blew his whistle before the girl with the braid had time to make her shot. He called a foul on Lara.

I trotted over and helped Cyndi to her feet.

"What's your problem?" Cyndi asked Lara.

"What did you do to her? To that girl we contacted?" Lara shot back.

"Nothing," Cyndi replied. She headed over to take her free-throw shot.

"I don't think she appeared for nothing," said Lara as she stepped into position as close to Cyndi as she could get. I stayed as close to Lara as I could. I wanted to hear everything either of them had to say about what happened at the séance.

Cyndi locked her eyes on the basket. She gave the ball a couple of bounces. Then a couple more. She seemed be having trouble getting focused.

"How did she die?" Lara asked. I don't know if anyone but Cyndi and me even heard her. But Cyndi definitely did. She let the ball go rolling across the floor. Chuck grabbed it and threw it to her.

"The guys said she killed herself," I answered. I hoped I could calm Lara down a little.

"You weren't even here when she died. But Cyndi was. Cyndi, how did she really die?" Lara pushed.

"She committed suicide. Everyone knows that," Cyndi burst out. "End of story!"

"Are we chatting or playing basketball here?" Danny called out.

"Shoot the ball," shouted the girl with the braid.

Cyndi bounced the ball. Took aim at the basket. Just as she released the basketball, Lara asked another question. "You killed her, didn't you, Cyndi? That's the truth, even if no one else knows it."

The ball went wild. Most of the kids went scrambling for it. Cyndi and Lara faced off. I stayed where I was.

"How can you say that?" Cyndi exclaimed.

"Because it explains how scared you were last night," cried Lara. "You wouldn't be afraid of Iris hurting you unless you hurt her first."

"You're crazy," Cyndi said. She turned away.

Lara charged forward and slammed her shoulder into Cyndi's back. *Skweeeet!* Chuck's whistle blasted again. "That's it!" he yelled. "Lara, you have schoolwork. I want you in the library working on it—now."

The gym went silent. Which was weird. At my school, if someone got some kind of punishment, there were always some "ooh's" and some "that's so unfair's" and some laughs. But every kid in the gym was absolutely silent as Lara walked out the double doors.

"Cyndi, you can go help get lunch ready," Chuck ordered.

"I didn't do any—," Cyndi began.

"I don't want to hear it," Chuck cut her off. "Go right now, please."

Now there was the noise I'd expected. At least some of it. Lots of talking. No laughing.

When Cyndi had left the gym, Chuck blew his whistle one more time. "Let's take a break and cool off. Heads and bodies. Be sure to drink some water. I don't want anyone passing out from dehydration."

I headed over to the cooler full of bottled water. This detention center was definitely upscale. The other time Frank and I had been "sentenced" to juvie, we'd had to clean our own latrines.

"I should get myself put in here," Maggie commented from her seat on the bleachers. "You guys are spending your Sunday playing basketball. I'm spending my Sunday locked in my mom's office doing extra-credit work, since I'm done with all my regular homework."

I raised one eyebrow at her. I'm kinda proud of my one-eyebrow technique.

"Okay, I'm not at this very minute doing the extra-credit work, but I'm supposed to be," Maggie said.

I sat down next to her. Maggie had made it clear

she knew a ton about every kid at Undercliff from snooping through her mother's files. Frank and I needed more info about Cyndi and Gregory. This seemed like a good time to get it.

"So you snuck out, huh?" I asked.

"Yep," said Maggie.

"What, you got bored of reading everybody's personal files?" I smiled at her. "I would have thought mine would have kept you fascinated."

I am so much better at this flirting thing than Frank is. There must be something about stammering and blushing that melts their hearts. Something close to seeing a kitty or a puppy or a bunny or some other soft, helpless creature.

Maggie laughed. "You and your brother are pretty ordinary. Maybe not out in the real world, but in here . . ." She shook her head. "You're nothing special."

Ouch. She hadn't said it in a mean way. But still. Ouch.

"Figuring out how to crack Auction House isn't exactly ordinary. It's not like any script kiddie could pull it off," I told her.

"You *did* get caught," Maggie reminded me.

"Everybody in here got caught," I reminded her.

"Yeah, but that hack Harlan did to get into every Clowney's electronic menu—that'll go down in history," Maggie said. "The guy's a genius. So is Danny, even though he ended up in here for assault. He's an idiot genius."

"You think one of the two of them is going to win the scholarship—the one in honor of Dr. Beirly's dad?" I asked.

"Without a doubt," she said. "They had some competition before Maryama and Gregory died. But now it's really down to the two of them."

Score. I'd confirmed that Gregory was a science head. Danny had motive for wanting him dead. He was competition. Actually, Harlan had the same motive. Maybe Harlan was creating the haunting to shut down Undercliff. Or maybe his motive was to win the scholarship. Maybe he had killed Maryama and Gregory and did all the other haunting stuff to create a smoke screen.

"Since you're all-knowing, what's the deal with Cyndi and Lara?" I asked. "Lara just got to Undercliff. How do she and Cyndi even know each other well enough to hate each other? Lara has to hate Cyndi to go around accusing her of murder."

Maggie shrugged. "People fight over nothing in here. I know there are movies, and basketball, and the food is decent and everything. But no one wants to be here, so everyone's already mad all the time. I saw two guys get into a fight once over who a plastic spoon belonged to. And they were standing next to a whole container of them."

"Dang," I muttered.

"Yeah," said Maggie. "It was—"

"Maggie!"

We both turned our head toward the voice. Dr. Nosek stood in the doorway of the gym. "How many times have we talked about—"

"I'm coming, I'm coming." Maggie gave me a little wave as she headed toward her mother, and what I guessed was all that extra-credit schoolwork.

I grabbed a bottle of water and walked over to the corner where Frank was hanging with a bunch of other kids, including Danny, Robert, and Harlan. The vibe was weird again. No one was laughing or joking around or trash talking. The group was quiet and solemn.

"The library is one of its places," the girl with the braid was saying. "I never go in there alone. I never go in there at all unless I have to for class."

"I can't believe Chuck sent Lara there. He knows Moses haunts that room. Everybody knows it," a guy with short brown hair commented. "That was sadistic of him."

"Lara doesn't even know that she should be on guard in there," added Harlan. "She's too new. I hadn't even shown her this yet." He pulled a couple of worn sheets of yellowed paper out of his pocket. Then he turned to me and Frank. "I wanted to show this to you guys too."

He handed the pieces of paper to Frank. I read over his shoulder.

Sometime in May, 1810
I have lost track of the date. I feel fortunate that I still recollect the month and year. Living here affects your mind, even if you were sane to begin with. No, I am still sane. I am Moses Bottelle. I will not scream. I am Moses Botelee. I am insane. I had three dogs—Posey, Jimmy, and Red. I could row a boat. I could whistle. I could play chess. I could weed. A woman named Charlotte wrote me letters. A woman named Charlotte loved me. These things are true. I am Moses.

I was put into the bag today, because I wouldnt eat my oatmeal after I found grubs in it. Is that not sane? The bag is supposed to help one regain his senses. I don't understand how. My doctor does not explain anything. Why should he, to a man he believes is out of his mind?

I don't know how long I was kept inside the bag. I know I felt as if the life were being sucked out of my body. I know I felt as if my throat and nose had been stuffed with cotton. I know I felt as if I could not draw breath. I know I was certain I was going to die.

I tried to concentrate on my happy memories, but they would not come to me in that dark, airless place. It is difficult to make them come to me now. I don't think I could survive a second treatment of the bag.

I did not scream. I stayed sane. I am Moses Bottelle.

"A couple of pieces of paper don't prove anything," Danny said. "Or maybe they prove a guy named Moses was a patient when this place was an asylum. But that's it. There's no proof he's haunting the library—or anyplace else."

"But you've seen things, right?" I asked.

I knew for sure he'd seen a ghost at the séance, but I didn't want to bring it up in front of everybody.

"I've seen what somebody wants me to see," Danny answered. "And so have the rest of you."

"How can you say that?" the girl with the braid demanded. "Gregory was your friend, and Moses killed him. Right in the library."

"Somebody killed him. I believe that," Danny retorted. "Just not any ghost. Gregory Teeter was murdered by a human. Probably someone who is in the building right now."

Fire?

I sat down for lunch at what had already become my usual table after one dinner and one breakfast at Undercliff. I scanned the room for Lara. Didn't see her at the food line or anywhere else. I did see Cyndi, though. She was already eating with some girls at a table near one of the windows.

"Shouldn't Lara be back from the library?" I asked the group. The regulars at my usual table were there too—Joe, Harlan, and Robert.

"I was just thinking that," said Robert. He craned his neck and did a search of the dinning hall. "Chuck is letting Cyndi eat with everyone. Lara should be in here too."

"Unless she showed some attitude. That could

have earned her some extra time," Danny commented.

"No one shows attitude if they're looking at library time," Harlan said.

"But you're the one who said that Lara doesn't know the deal about the library yet," Robert reminded him.

"Yeah, but I was thinking about it," Harlan said. "Lara would feel Moses's spirit right away. She's, you know, *sensitive* like that."

"Rat poop," muttered Danny.

"When are you going to just admit you were wrong?" Harlan asks. "Ghosts do exist. You got proof last night."

"That wasn't proof of anything," Danny told him.

"What is wrong with you? She was there. Right in front of us," Harlan insisted.

Danny shook his head. "Magicians a hundred and fifty years ago were making their audiences see ghosts. Are you telling me if I challenged you to make a spirit appear as one of your pranks, you couldn't do it?"

Danny and Harlan were starting to sound kind of like me and Joe.

"Yeah, *I* could do it. But I wasn't doing it last night. And there weren't any eighteenth-century magicians around either," Harlan answered.

"What about that girl Cyndi?" I asked. "Does she have the chops to pull off an illusion like that?"

Harlan snorted.

"No possible way," said Danny. "The girl is D-U-M dumb."

"And why would Cyndi want to create an image of a girl who hated her?" Robert asked.

"What was the deal with Cyndi and Iris?" Joe cut in, before anyone could answer Robert's question. "Did you guys know Iris? Did the ghost—or whatever—even look like her? Or was Cyndi just flipping?"

"Looked exactly like her," said Robert.

Harlan nodded.

"Like I said last night, I never talked to the girl or anything. But yeah, the illusion looked like her," Danny agreed.

"I can think of only one reason Iris might be mad at Cyndi," Robert volunteered. "Dr. Beirly was having Cyndi do some letters for him on the computer."

"Cause she was Beirly's little pet. I know that much," added Danny.

"And I guess Cyndi caught Iris snooping around in his office one day," Robert continued.

"And of course she told Beirly, because that's

what pets do." Harlan picked up the story. "There were rumors going around that Beirly was going to ship Iris off to Allendale."

"Allendale?" Robert burst out. "I never heard that. I didn't even know they took girls. I've seen guys cry when they got sentenced there."

"Some people think that's why she offed herself," said Harlan. "Because she'd rather be dead than end up over there."

Robert leaned forward. "Whoa. So maybe Iris really does blame Cyndi for her death. If she killed herself because she was getting sent to Allendale, and she never would have gotten sent to Allendale if Cyndi hadn't gone to Beirly with what she saw . . ."

"You're piling up a lot of 'ifs' there," I commented.

"Maybe Iris just appeared because she wanted an apology from Cyndi. Cyndi got all flipped out, but Iris never said she was there to get revenge on Cyndi or anything," Robert said.

"Iris didn't actually say anything about Cyndi. All she said was, 'Somebody hurt me,'" Joe reminded everyone.

"Well, Cyndi didn't act like she thought Iris was just dropping in to say hi," Harlan said.

"It makes sense that Cyndi was feeling guilty

for ratting out Iris. That's why—" Danny's words were cut off by a series of long, loud beeps.

"Another fire drill." Robert scarfed down one more bite of his hot dog and stood up.

"I don't think it's a drill," said Joe. "Unless they pipe in smoke to make the drills more realistic." He jerked his chin toward the kitchen door. Snakes of smoke were drifting through the cracks and into the dining hall.

"Everybody, calmly and quietly out to the front lawn. Calmly and quietly!" Micah called out from the back of the room.

"Come on, everyone. Let's go," Chuck added, clapping his hands. Most of the staff was helping herd the kids outside, including Dr. Nosek, with Maggie in tow.

The smoke was thicker in the hall. I pulled the top of my T-shirt up over my mouth and nose as a filter. I had to keep blinking to keep my eyes clear.

"The ghost is doing this!" the girl with the braid cried. "It's tired of picking us off one by one. It wants us all dead right now."

"Shut up, Samantha," somebody answered.

"No, she's right!" someone else joined in.

"Where's the heat?" Joe asked me.

Good point. There was a ton of smoke. But no

heat. Could we be that far away from the source of the fire?

"No running!" Micah called from somewhere behind us. He coughed a couple of times, then continued. "When you get outside, walk all the way to the edge of the grass."

Once I'd made it through the main exit, I pulled my shirt off my face and sucked in a lungful of the fresh air. Much better.

"And where are the flames?" Joe asked when we hit the edge of the grass.

I turned and studied the massive Undercliff building. I saw a lot of smoke pouring out of the windows of the kitchen and dining hall. But no flames. No flickering light, even.

"Get in a straight line," Dr. Nosek called. "I need to check you all off on my clipboard." Maggie stood next to her, smirking.

I was hit with a memory: Maggie talking to me about the three little bones of the ear. She'd moved closer to me—and I'd smelled candy and something pungent.

"Saltpeter and sucrose," I muttered.

"What?" asked Joe.

"Saltpeter and sucrose," I repeated.

"Would it kill you to just use the word smoke bomb?" Joe complained.

I pulled him away from the others so we wouldn't be overheard. "I was remembering that yesterday Maggie smelled like candy and something that made the inside of my nose twitch. And she's looking pretty happy right now. Plus no heat, no flame."

Joe spotted her and nodded his head. "She looks like a cat who just ate a canary dipped in cream sauce," he said, using one of Aunt Trudy's favorite expressions.

"I think we need to put Maggie on our suspect list," I said. I had to talk a little louder to be heard over the howl of the fire engine's siren.

"She's not happy spending time at Undercliff, that's for sure," Joe agreed. "Who knows how far she'd go to get some payback for having to spend every free hour here."

"From what Harlan was saying at lunch yesterday, she has the science background you'd need to pull off some complex illusions," I commented.

SUSPECT PROFILE

Name: Maggie Nosek

Hometown: Glastonbury, Connecticut

Physical description: 5'4", approximately 120 lbs., age 15, red hair, hazel eyes.

Occupation: Student

"So she goes on the list," Joe said. "But we're keeping the ghost on there too."

"Oh, I was talking to Maggie in the gym," Joe said. "She told me that Gregory Teeter was also a front-runner for the scholarship. So that beefs up Danny and Harlan's motive for killing him."

"Danny's the one who really seems to care about the scholarship. He sees it as a way to get a whole new life. But Harlan might want to win just as bad. We don't know," I mused.

"Maggie's motive seems like the weakest of the three of them. It's hard to imagine her taking out two guys just because she's teed off at her mom," Joe commented.

"Yeah. Although we've seen stranger motives," I reminded him.

"Maybe Gregory's death was an accident. Then

maybe Maggie felt like she had to continue the hauntings to keep the attention on the ghost, not her," suggested Joe.

"And so she killed Maryama to cover up the first death?" I asked.

Joe shrugged. "Sometimes it feels like we're going to have to put our whole yearlong sentence in at Undercliff to figure this all out."

"Here comes Elton," I told him. Elton walked away from one of the firemen and over to the ragged line of kids at the edge of the lawn.

"False alarm," he announced. "I guess that old saying 'where there's smoke there's fire' is wrong. All we've got here is smoke from some ingenious smoke bombs."

Maggie laughed. She wasn't the only one. Harlan practically fell down, he was laughing so hard.

"If anyone has anything to tell me about how to make a smoke bomb—which I've never done—I'd love to hear it," Elton continued. He returned to the firemen.

"We need to stay out here a little longer to let the smoke clear," Dr. Nosek announced. "But I've got you all checked off, so you can walk around if you want to."

"You think we should try to talk to Maggie?" asked Joe. "Hey, wait! Look over there. It's Lara. I want to see if anything happened while she was in the library." He took off across the grass. I followed him. He could have waited to see what I wanted to do. But whatever.

"So did you feel anything in the library?" Joe asked Lara. "I don't know if you'd heard, but that's supposed to be one of Moses's favorite spots."

I noticed that Lara's face was pale, and her breathing seemed accelerated. "Are you feeling okay?" I asked.

"That's what I was coming over here to ask," Micah said, appearing next to me. "Lara, if you need to go in and lie down, that's not a problem. There's no smoke up in the dorm."

"No, I'm all right," she said quickly. "I'd rather stay out here, with everybody."

"Are you sure?" Micah pressed, his expression grim.

"Yeah. Completely sure," Lara told him.

"I'm going to talk to Elton about what happened. It's unacceptable. Why doesn't he get that?" Micah clearly wasn't expecting an answer. He turned and left, heading toward Elton.

"Something did happen," said Joe.

"Yeah, you could say that," Lara agreed.

"Tell us," I urged.

"I've got to sit," she answered. "I feel like all my

muscles have been snipped. Like they aren't connected to my bones anymore."

"Over there." I nodded toward a bench by a tree that had already dropped a lot more leaves on the ground.

"It was hideous," Lara admitted as soon as she was settled on the bench. "I never . . . I can't even describe it."

"Start at the beginning," Joe suggested. "Just take it step by step."

Lara pulled in a long, shuddering breath. "Okay. Okay. I went into the library, and I got a magazine from the rack, because I didn't feel like doing homework. I was all by myself, which was kind of cool. You know how it is here, you're with other people practically every second."

Joe and I nodded.

"So, I'm reading, and the lights go out. Which is no biggie. It's just a room with no light," Lara continued. She rubbed her arms with her hands. "But then I started feeling weird. Or maybe I was feeling weird before the lights went out. I don't remember." She stared blankly out at the gray stones of Undercliff.

"Then what?" I prompted.

"Then it was like the walls were closing in. I didn't see them moving or anything. But that's how it felt. Like they were tightening around me.

Squeezing the air out of me." She started gasping.

"Lots of air out here," Joe told her. "No walls at all."

"Right." Lara tried to smile, but couldn't quite pull it off. "So I was suffocating. I wanted to yell for help, but I didn't have enough air. Then I heard this other voice begging for help. A man. Begging to be let out. And gasping for breath. Gasping and wheezing." She pressed her hand against her throat.

"Could you see anyone?" I asked.

"No. The man sounded so close. I should have been able to see him, even with it being so dark. But I couldn't. I could just hear him pleading for help. Then I guess I blacked out," Lara related. "The next thing I remember is Beirly leaning over me. The lights were back on."

"Intense," Joe said.

"Uh, yeah," Lara agreed. "He asked me all these questions and took my pulse and everything. Then he said that I'd had a panic attack. He said that the feeling of smothering was a common symptom. Shortness of breath, too. He thought I probably hyperventilated and passed out for a few seconds."

"You don't think that could have been it?" I asked.

"No. No way," Lara insisted. "I heard that voice. It was real. I never believed in that stuff before, but something was in that room with me. A presence."

"Never believed?" Joe burst out. "What about the séance?"

"I believe in ghosts," Lara said quickly. "That's not what I meant. I meant I never believed all that stuff people say about spirits attacking humans. I always thought anything that appeared like an attack was just an attempt by a ghost to communicate."

"Maybe the ghost was trying to communicate," Joe told her. "You said it was begging for help."

"It wasn't asking me for help," Lara insisted. "It was dying. It was suffocating. And it was like if he was going to die, he wanted me to die too. He wanted me to die!"

Call 911

"How did you know that, Danny?" Harlan burst out. "That was a grad school–level question."

"You know what I know?" Danny answered. "I know it's Danny five, Harlan one."

We were all back in the common room after the non-fire. Things were already getting back to normal. Danny and Harlan were quizzing each other on science questions, prepping for the test that would determine who got the scholarship. Lara, Robert, Frank, the girl with the braid—I found out her name was Samantha—and I were playing poker. Cyndi and a couple of other kids were watching TV on the other side of the room.

I checked my hand. Yeah, it was just as bad as I

remembered. But I decided to go all in anyway. I wanted out of the game—and out of the common room. It would be hard for Frank and me to both get out of the room. But I figured that maybe I'd have a shot at it flying solo.

Frank called. Somehow he always knows when I'm bluffing.

Robert giggled—yes, giggled—when he saw my hand. I had a seven as my high card. And nothing else.

Samantha scooped away the pot. There was no money in it. Undercliff might have been a totally cushy detention center, but not that cushy. We were playing for packets of sugar. "It's off to the Loser's Lounge for you, my friend," she told me.

"That's okay," I said. "I'm not feeling that good, anyway."

Frank shot me a sharp look. Somehow he always knows when I'm lying, too.

"Maybe inhaling all that smoke made you sick," said Robert.

"Or losing all that sugar," Lara commented.

"I think I'm going to ask Micah if I can go lie down for a little while," I said. I could almost hear Playback going "Wimp, wimp, wimp!" But I wasn't being wimpy. I was being covert. It was still kind of embarrassing, though.

"Are you sure?" Frank asked. "It doesn't seem like it's a good idea to go anywhere in this place by yourself. With the ghosts and everything."

Translation: Are you sure you don't need big brother to get your back?

And actually, I would like big brother to get my back. But as I said, I didn't think we were both going to talk ourselves out of the common room.

"I'll be fine," I answered, then headed over to Micah and gave him my sad story. He didn't seem to have any kind of lie-o-meter installed. "Of course you should go get some rest," he told me. "Do you think you need to go to the infirmary?"

"No, I'm just a little queasy. I'm sure it's from the smoke," I answered.

"Things are getting out of hand here," said Micah. It seemed like he was talking pretty much to himself. Then his focus flipped back to me. "I could get you a couple of aspirin. That could help."

"Really, I just need to crash for a little bit," I assured him.

"Not a problem. I'll just sign you out. And I'll come check on you in a while," Micah said.

That would limit the time I had. But I could do some digging. "Thanks," I told him. I headed out of the room, making sure not to walk too fast, since I was feeling illish and all.

I started toward the stairs, then looped around and headed for the administration offices. They were on the first floor, in the opposite wing from the kitchen, dining hall, and common room. Except for Beirly's office. He had the big one upstairs on the third floor.

It didn't take long to find Dr. Nosek's office. And I was in luck. Maggie was inside. Alone. Twirling back and forth in her mom's rolling desk chair.

"Hey," I said as I stepped inside.

Maggie flashed me a grin. "Just admit it. You think I'm cute. That's so why you're here."

"I admit it," I said. She might as well think I was here to keep flirting. And anyway, she was cute.

"So what does your brother think?" she asked.

Oh, please. This again.

"You should know that my brother has this condition that makes it almost physically impossible to speak to a female between the ages of thirteen and twenty," I told her. "So unless you want to spend a lot of time staring at him, you should—"

"Staring at him doesn't sound too bad," Maggie interrupted.

"So you want me to leave?" I turned toward the door. "Because I could just leave."

"No. Stay. Please. Please, please, please," Maggie begged, pressing her hands against her heart in this super-dramatic—and pretty cute—way. "I was about to die of boredom. I'm three months into my sentence. Every day after school I have to come right here. Every weekend that my mom works, which is three weekends a month, I have to come here. I'm going crazy."

"Is that why you set off the smoke bomb?" I asked.

Sometimes it's good to surprise a suspect. At least I think so. It's not Frank's style. He wouldn't have confronted Maggie unless he had absolute, concrete proof that she'd set the smoke bomb. But I figured her reaction would tell me a lot.

"I'm not the delinquent in the room," Maggie said, smirking. "It's a lot more likely that you did it."

"Come on. You're the one who said you're sentenced here," I reminded her. "It's not like you've never gotten into any trouble. Besides, yesterday at lunch, you reeked."

Actually, Frank's the one who had noticed the odor on her. Good thing we share all our intel.

Maggie stood up, her body getting tense. "What are you—"

This time I interrupted her. "You were giving off fumes—candy and rotten eggs. I put it together when the fire turned out to be fake."

Okay, yeah, Frank put it together. But I thought it was a more effective interrogation technique if I said I was the one who connected the dots.

"It was pretty cool," I added.

Maggie's shoulders relaxed. "Yeah. That's what my mother gets for letting me set up a chemistry lab in the empty office next door."

And . . . confession.

"She's going to be sorry she let me in the door of this place," Maggie continued. "I figure if she's going to treat me like I'm one of the delinquents— sorry—I might as well act like one. She even makes me have sessions with Dr. Beirly. Do you believe that?"

"Elton seemed okay," I answered. "But I wouldn't want to have to talk to a psychiatrist who was my mom's boss. That's pretty weird."

"Yeah, and he's gotten my mom all freaked just because I like scary movies and roller coasters and watching *Shark Week* on TV," Maggie told me.

"I worship *Shark Week*," I told her.

"See, and you're normal," she said.

"Except for the part where a judge sent me here to pay my debt to society," I agreed.

Maggie laughed. Then she shook her head, making her curly red hair bounce. "It's not funny. Beirly is making my mom nuts. Ever since I started having therapy sessions with him, she acts like she thinks I'm dangerous or something. Like I might just go off and—" Maggie made an exploding noise. "I hate the guy. He's ruining my life. Or at least he's convinced my mother that *she* needs to ruin my life. Actually, I hate them both. But I hate him a little more."

"O-kay," I said. "I'm making a mental note never to get you mad." It did seem like a good idea to keep Maggie calm. She was moving up on my mental suspect list.

I figured I still had a little more time before Micah might come and check on me. "Would it be okay if I use your mom's computer for a couple of minutes?" I asked.

"It would be okay with me if you threw it on the floor and stomped on it," Maggie said cheerfully. She pushed the desk chair toward me. I sat down and rolled myself up to the computer.

Just because Maggie set off the smoke bomb, it didn't mean she'd killed anybody or even done any of the other things to make Undercliff seem haunted. The ghost was still on my list of suspects for that bag of badness. Moses the ghost, I mean. It seemed like Iris the ghost was a new player. Nobody had mentioned a ghost like her in the stories about all the haunted spots in the detention center. Everybody always talked about a patient from the insane asylum.

If Lara was right, the way to stop Moses was to find out what he wanted and to help him get it. I figured a little research on Moses when he was alive would be a good place to start.

I googled Undercliff Insane Asylum and got a bunch of hits. I checked out the first one. It had drawings of a lot of the devices I'd already heard about—like that spinning chair and the bag.

I wanted to read all the details, but there wasn't time. I needed specific info about Moses, so I went back and googled "Undercliff Insane Asylum Moses Bottelle." I got some hits that included "Undercliff Insane Asylum" and "Moses," but not "Bottelle." I clicked on one. It had a list of patients and the years they were at the asylum. There was a Moses Goodman, from 1864 to 1892.

But there was no Moses Bottelle.

In any year.

That was definitely info I needed to pass on to Frank. Where had the journal entries come from if there was no Moses? Obviously they had to be fakes, but who had faked them?

"Find the next site you want to crack?" asked Maggie.

"Nope." I quickly clicked the Undercliff Asylum

site closed. "I'm reformed, remember? Which reminds me—I should get back. I don't want to get in trouble."

"You definitely don't want to get assigned to have any chats with Beirly," Maggie said.

"True that." I took off, heading for the dorm. But I decided I had time for a quick detour. I wanted to take a look at the library.

Well, "wanted" might not be exactly the right word. Admit it—Lara's story was pretty danged creepy. But I needed to check it out. The room might hold a piece of evidence that would help me and Frank crack this case wide open.

It also might hold a ghost, I thought as I stepped inside the library. Although probably not the ghost of Moses Bottelle. Since he'd never set foot in Undercliff.

It was a small room. Four or five high rows of books. A couple of long wooden tables, and—

Suddenly it was like there wasn't enough air in the room. I was breathing, but I just wasn't getting enough oxygen.

There was a body on the floor next to the table farthest away from me. I raced over there and dropped to my knees. Danny. It was Danny lying there.

His eyes wide with fear. Lips pulled back in a snarl.

I gave him a light shake. "Danny, can you hear me? Danny!"

No response.

I tilted his head back and listened for breathing. Nothing.

Okay. I had to start CPR.

I pinched Danny's nose closed and leaned forward to breathe into his mouth. I still felt like I didn't have enough breath to keep my own lungs filled. "Here we go," I muttered.

Then I caught a flash of movement to the left. I jerked my head in that direction. And saw Harlan staring at me.

"Harlan, go call 911. Right now!" I ordered. "Danny's not breathing."

He blinked a couple of times, then turned and dashed off. I blew into Danny's mouth until I saw his chest rise, then got ready to give another breath.

One thought kept ripping through my brain. *Did I just ask Danny's murderer to help me save his life?*

Let Me Out

"**D**anny's not breathing!" Harlan shouted as he burst into the common room. "We've got to call 911."

I was on my feet before he got the last word out.

"What?" Micah exclaimed. "What happened?"

"I don't know. I don't know," Harlan answered. "We were in the library. Studying like you told us we could. I went to get a book from the dorm. When I came back, Joe was giving him CPR."

"Chuck!" called Micah.

"Already on it," Chuck answered from across the room, holding up his cell phone.

Micah turned and bolted out of the room. I

was right behind him. "Frank, stay down here," he ordered.

"I know CPR," I told him. "Maybe I can help." I definitely wasn't leaving Joe up in the library without backup. It sounded like our killer had gone after Danny. The killer could still be in the library—with Joe.

We scrambled up the stairs and into the library. I immediately spotted Joe working on Danny. I estimated he'd put in about two minutes, and it didn't look like he'd gotten any response yet.

I rushed over and got into position next to Joe. "I'll take over the chest compressions."

Joe nodded. Blew a breath into Danny's mouth. Another one. I watched Danny's chest rise and fall.

Then I got my hands into position and began pressing down on his chest. Fast. About two times per second. Pressing his chest down about two inches each time.

Micah jerked open the nearest window. "Some fresh air might help," he said. He opened another window.

After thirty compressions, Joe gave Danny two more breaths. We repeated the pattern again and again. Then I heard the EMTs rushing into the room. "Are you guys okay? Can you keep it up while we get the defibrillator set up?" one of them asked us.

"No problem," answered Joe.

"Okay, we got it," the same EMT said about thirty seconds later. Joe and I backed off. The two EMTs got Danny's shirt open, wiped his chest dry, and attached the defibrillator pads—one to the upper right section of his chest, one to the lower left.

"Clear!" the other EMT called out. Then he hit the shock button.

Danny's body jerked.

"Do we have a pulse?" the first EMT asked.

"No, we're going to have to go again," his partner answered. "Clear!" He hit the shock button.

Danny's body jerked. My body jerked a little too, just watching.

"We got something," the second EMT announced. Then I heard Danny suck in a breath.

Joe and I grinned at each other. "What's his name?" asked the first EMT.

"Danny," Joe, Micah, and I answered together.

"Danny, you're okay," the first EMT said. "We're just going to roll you over on your side, get you a little more comfortable." He and his partner gently moved Danny into the standard recovery position.

"What happened, Danny?" Joe burst out.

"I don't think he should be talking," said Micah.

"He needs to be still and rest," the second EMT agreed.

"It was here," Danny gasped out. "Just like Lara said. The ghost . . ."

I was definitely thinking about the ghost when Joe and I snuck back into the library about eleven that night. And I know I said I don't believe in ghosts. And it's true. But come on. Anyone who had been in the room when Danny almost died would be thinking of ghosts right now. He pretty much said a ghost had tried to kill him.

"You're creeped out. Admit it," Joe whispered. "You think the ghost could be in here."

I hate when he does that. When he crawls into my head like that. I didn't answer. I didn't want to give him the satisfaction of knowing he was right. And I didn't want to lie.

"Not answering is the same as admitting it," Joe told me.

I really hate when he does that.

"Let's just do what we're here to do," I muttered. "Look for evidence."

"Of the natural or supernatural kind," Joe agreed.

We divided the room in half, then I divided mine into quadrants. I find it more effective to search a space in small squares. It helps me see more when I don't try to look at too much at once.

My first quadrant contained a chair, part of a

table, a section of floor, a section of wall, and a section of ceiling. I took my time, checking for any abnormalities, anything that seemed out of place or that didn't belong at all. And I tried not to think about ghosts. I needed every particle of my brain matter focused on the search.

Danny had almost died tonight. Lara might have come close to dying this afternoon. Joe and I had to crack this case fast. Everyone at Undercliff was in life-threatening danger.

Well, except the killer.

I noticed a small, dark smudge on the wall and moved in for a better look. Up close, I could see that the smudge had a wavy print. *Could be from the toe of a sneaker,* I thought. Too tapered for any other part. Although it was a weird place for a shoe mark. Way too high.

It made me feel a little better when I came to the conclusion that a ghost foot probably wouldn't have left a scuff mark. According to the whacked-out shows Joe watched, I should be seeing a blob of slimy ectoplasm if I was dealing with something from the other side. "Hey, J—"

The word evaporated in my mouth. Along with all my saliva. Because the sound of someone breathing— no, gasping for breath—was filling the room. The entire room.

"Heeelp," a voice wheezed. "Let me out. I can't . . . Pleassse."

"I found part of a sound system," Joe announced.

"Let me . . ." The ghostly voice cut out.

"One of the books on this shelf is hollow," Joe continued. "There's a tiny tape recorder inside. Sounds like there are speakers in multiple locations."

I cleared my throat. "Yeah. The voice sounded like it was coming from everywhere at once," I agreed.

"Are you going to admit it now?" Joe asked, walking over to me. "Just admit it. For at least one second there, you totally believed in ghosts."

"Okay, okay, for a second," I admitted, because I knew he'd never let it go until I did. "But what about you? Do you think a ghost went to Circuit City and bought that tape recorder? Or do you think we're dealing with an actual living human here?"

Joe rolled his eyes. "I think an actual living human tried to kill Danny. And probably Maryama and Gregory too. I'm still not sure what happened at the séance with that Iris girl. I mean ghost."

I sighed. "One thing at a time. Check this out." I pointed to the smudge.

"Huh." Joe touched it lightly with one finger. "It's almost like somebody braced their foot up here. Although it would be pretty much impossible to reach this spot from the ground."

I climbed up on the closest table. I could definitely touch the spot where the scuff mark was with my foot from up here.

"Check out that group of ceiling tiles almost over your head," Joe told me. "The holes in them are a little bigger than the holes in the other tiles."

I studied the ceiling. Joe was right. This room had to have been renovated at some point. Back when Undercliff was the asylum, it definitely didn't have acoustical ceiling tiles. Handy for keeping the spooky ghost sound effects from leaking out. I wondered if that had been the plan.

Using one of my lock-picking tools, I carefully pried off a couple of the tiles Joe had pointed out. "You have to get a look at this," I told my brother.

Joe climbed up on the table next to me. We both stared up at the cross Ts of the suspended ceilings. The original ceiling was about four feet above it. Several silver tanks rested on the Ts.

"Oxygen tanks?" I said, thinking out loud. "That doesn't make sense."

Joe jumped up, grabbed one of the Ts, and pulled himself up for a closer look. He pressed his foot against the wall for balance. The tip of his sneaker ended up less than a foot away from the scuff mark.

"Not oxygen," he told me. "They're helium tanks. And they're set up to pump helium through the oversize holes in the tiles."

"Helium. That makes total sense," I said.

Joe let himself drop back to the table. "Right. When you take helium into your lungs, it messes up the way they exchange gases."

"Oxygen is actually taken out of your lungs," I agreed. "If you wanted to make somebody feel like they were suffocating without actually stuffing them in the bag, making them breathe helium would do it."

"Oh, man," exclaimed Joe. "When I first came into the room and found Danny, I felt like I couldn't breathe. I thought it was 'cause I was freaked, seeing him lying there. I thought he was dead at first. But it had to have been the helium. Then when you and Micah came in, Micah opened some windows. . . ."

"Every time somebody has had a ghost encounter in here, it's been a combination of the sound system and the helium," I said. "I guess usually the helium is cut off in time."

"In time to scare whoever's in here out of their skin. Like Lara," Joe remarked.

"But whoever's behind this almost killed somebody today," I said.

"It would have been the third time." Joe handed

me one of the ceiling tiles. "We'd better get these back in place. We don't want our 'ghost' to know that we're on to some of its methods."

"Pretty good methods too." I slid the tile into place, and Joe handed me another one. "Helium would be almost impossible to detect in an autopsy. It makes sense the coroner came up with the dying-from-fear theory."

"Let's get out of here," Joe said when we had the ceiling back together.

"I'm definitely ready." We climbed off the table and headed out into the hall. Almost immediately I heard voices.

Definitely human. Micah for sure.

"I swear to you I'm not going to take anymore," Micah yelled from what I assumed was Beirly's office.

"You don't really have a choice," a man answered. I was almost positive it was Beirly. I hadn't heard his voice as often as Micah's, though.

"There are always choices, Elton," Micah shot back.

Definitely Beirly, then.

"Of course. You're right. But we both know the smart choice is for you to be a good boy and follow orders. And we both know why," Beirly stated.

"That's what you think," Micah snapped. "But

135

things have changed since I first came here. I know exactly how to shut this place down. I can do it whenever I want to. And I will if you make me. I'll shut Undercliff down."

Somebody Murdered Me

"So that was quite the *discussion* between Micah and Elton," I said. Frank and I were back in the bathroom off the boys' dorm. We have way too many conversations in bathrooms. At least in my opinion. Who knows? Frank may dig it.

"I think Micah definitely has to go on our suspect list." Frank squirted some of the nasty pink soap powder on his hands and started to wash up. I figured I hadn't gotten all that dirty exploring the library's drop ceiling.

"He could be our ghost," I agreed. "He told Elton he'd shut Undercliff down. Haunting the place could do it."

"Haunting the place and murdering people,"

Frank reminded me. Like I needed reminding.

SUSPECT PROFILE

Name: Micah Neel

Hometown: Fargo, North Dakota

Physical description: 6'2", approximately 175 lbs., age 26, sandy hair, gray eyes.

Occupation: Coordinator, Undercliff Detention Center

Background: High school dropout. Only kid in family who didn't go to college.

Suspicious behavior: Threatened to shut down Undercliff.

Suspected of: Murders of Maryama Soll and Gregory Teeter; attempted murder of Danny Laybourn.

Possible motive: Angry at Elton Beirly.

"I wonder what he was so mad at Elton about," I said.

"That's definitely on our things-to-find-out list," Frank answered. "Beirly makes Micah deal with his dry cleaning, but it has to be something bigger than that."

"Oh, hey, I talked to Maggie before I went to the library and got kind of caught up trying to save Danny's life," I told him. "Turns out Maggie isn't exactly a Dr. Beirly fan either."

"That's interesting," Frank commented. "Why not?"

"Her mom makes her have psychiatry sessions with him, and I guess he thinks watching scary movies and going on scary rides at amusement parks and stuff like that is bad for her. So her mother doesn't want her doing anything fun," I explained. "Maggie's not exactly a fan of her mother, either. But we already knew that."

"Did you find anything out about the smoke bombs?" Frank asked.

"What am I, an amateur?" I shot back. "It's confirmed. Maggie set the smoke bombs. I got her to confess. I didn't have to use my bright light or bring you in to do the good Hardy/bad Hardy routine on her."

"The helium tanks are pretty light. And Maggie seems to have access to the entire place," said Frank.

"She's supposed to stay in her mom's office, but she definitely doesn't," I agreed.

"So she could have gotten the tanks and the sound system set up in the library," Frank continued.

"Micah too. And Harlan," I added, running down our suspect list. "I guess Danny's off the list—unless we have two ghost masters who aren't working together. Or unless he's fiendishly clever and wanted to throw us off the track, so he almost offed himself."

"He got pretty close to dead just to mislead us," said Frank.

"That's the fiendish part of it," I told him.

"We have Beirly on the list too," Frank reminded me. "He almost seems to encourage people to think Undercliff is haunted."

"Bringing in that psychic and everything. And not keeping it all secret." I nodded. "Plus he definitely has access to the whole place. What do you think we should do—"

I didn't have time to finish my question. Harlan interrupted by coming into the bathroom. "Here you guys are," he said. "Come on. Lara decided we have to have another séance tonight. She says the psychic energy at Undercliff is about to boil over, and we need to try to calm it down."

"I'm not going," Frank said.

"What?" I demanded.

"Danny was almost killed by a ghost not even a day ago. Not even half a day," Frank explained. "I'm not going to go invite the ghost to come out and play. That's insane."

Okay, now I knew Frank had some kind of plan going. He knew for sure a ghost hadn't had anything to do with what happened to Danny.

"She's not going to try to contact Moses," Harlan said. "She wants to talk to Iris again. Lara's worried about her."

Frank let out a groan. "I don't want to talk to any ghost of any kind." He turned to me. "I think you should stay away too. But it's not like you ever listen to what I think. So just go ahead and go. I know you will anyway." He headed out of the bathroom.

Message received. Frank wanted me to go to the séance.

"If you're coming, come on," Harlan told me. "Lara, Robert, and Cyndi are waiting in the hall."

"Cyndi's doing the séance again?" I shook my head. "How did that happen?"

"Lara said if Cyndi isn't the one who hurt Iris, Cyndi doesn't need to worry about being there when Iris appears again," Harlan explained. "Basically, she made it sound like if Cyndi bailed, then

Cyndi was the one Iris was talking about. The one who hurt her."

"I hope we don't have to break up a girl-ghost catfight," I said.

Harlan snorted. "I think your brother's right. I think we're both nuts to be doing this." But he led the way out to the hall, and I followed him. Without Danny to pick the lock—I didn't want to show off my ATAC-taught skills—we risked the main staircase.

Maybe Elton and Micah were still up on the third floor, fighting. We definitely didn't see or hear anybody and got safely inside the chapel. Not that getting in was really the part I was worried about.

Frank has a plan, I told myself. I knew he'd be around to get my back if I needed it.

"You know what to do, everybody," Lara said softly. "Let's make the circle and charge the candles."

We sat down at the front of the chapel the way we had before, and Lara passed the candles around so they could absorb our good vibes. We'd been a circle of seven last time. Now we were five. It felt a lot smaller.

"Isn't there something we can do to protect ourselves?" Cyndi asked as Lara poured a small pile of cinnamon in front of her. "We do things to welcome ghosts and make them feel comfortable. But what about us? Isn't there a smell they hate that we could use if things go wrong?"

"If something goes wrong, we break the circle, and I ask the spirit to leave," Lara answered. "I told you, you don't have anything to worry about. Unless you're the one who hurt Iris." She turned and looked straight at Cyndi. "If you are, you have to tell me now. I won't be able to protect you from her if you don't tell me everything."

"There's nothing to tell!" Cyndi burst out, her voice climbing. "I didn't like her, okay? I thought she was a little sneak. And she didn't like me. She thought I was a priss, I guess. But I didn't do anything. She killed herself. I didn't do anything to her."

Whoa. Just whoa.

"You pretty much got her sent to Allendale," Harlan burst out. "By going to Beirly about her snooping around in his office."

Cyndi shrugged. "I told what she *did*. If she killed herself because she didn't want to face her punishment, I don't consider it my responsibility."

Lara gave a small, tight smile. "If you're not responsible for hurting Iris, then you have nothing to worry about." She patted Cyndi's hand. "You're doing a good thing, trying to bring Iris peace, even if you weren't friends."

"You forced me to be here. Let's get it over with," Cyndi said, jerking away.

"All right. Join hands. Focus on the candle flames. And let your mind go blank," Lara instructed.

I took Lara's hand. It was cool, but I could feel the tension in her muscles. Cyndi took my other hand. Her fingers were slick with sweat and trembling.

Blanking out my mind was even harder than the last time. And not because I was thinking about ice cream. Because I was thinking about what happened last time. Because I was waiting for it to happen again.

"Concentrate," Lara coached. "Use the flame and your own breathing to guide you."

I focused on the feel of the air moving in and out of my lungs. Didn't help. It made me think of Danny. And that suffocating sensation I felt in the library.

Candles. Forget the breathing, just look at the candles, I told myself. I did what I could, and eventually Lara began to speak.

"Our beloved Iris, we ask that you commune with us and move among us," she said. "Our beloved Iris, we ask that you commune with us and move among us."

"The mist," Robert whispered.

I looked behind me. The mist had already begun to form.

And then she was there. Iris. Light shimmering around her in a halo. In that same dress—white with little purple flowers. It blew around her legs. Her hair blew around her face. It was like she was standing in a wind that only she could feel.

"Someone murdered me," she said.

I'd been expecting that hideous rusty squeal. But her voice was as clear and sweet as it had become by the end of the last séance.

"Someone murdered me. And someone must pay."

There was a long pause. I wanted to answer her, to promise her that I would discover who killed her no matter what. But somehow I couldn't get my mouth to open.

"No one killed you, Iris!" Cyndi cried. "You killed yourself, remember? It was you! It wasn't me or anyone else. It was you!"

"Someone murdered me," the spirit said again. "And someone must pay. Blood for my blood."

The Mist

The tiny hairs on the back of my neck stood straight up when Iris said, "Blood for my blood."

Iris didn't say it, I reminded myself. *Iris is dead. Someone is using the idea of her, of her death, for their own sick reasons. That's why you're here. To find out who and why.*

I'd crept into the chapel while Lara was having the group focus on the candles. I figured that was my best shot for getting in unseen. It had worked—although things had started up faster than they had at the last séance.

"Whose blood, Iris?" Lara called. "Who killed you?"

"I said nobody!" Cyndi snapped. But she sounded more scared than angry. A lot more scared.

I crawled down the floor in front of one of the pews. I'd chosen this pew because I thought it was in the section of the room the mist had come from during the last séance. Mist was pumping out from someplace nearby this time too, which was lucky for me. It meant I was close to the source, plus the mist would help keep me hidden.

"Quiet, Cyndi. I'm the only one who is allowed to talk to the spirit," Lara told her. "Iris, who killed you?"

I couldn't see anything but the mist. I couldn't see Iris—the image of Iris, I mean. But clearly the group up front could. I reached the end of the pew. I swallowed hard a couple of times to keep from coughing. The mist was really thick here. But I hadn't spotted what was generating it.

Maybe the next pew down. I slid under the wooden bench and felt something sharp cut into my back. Something too sharp to be the underside of a pew.

"Someone here knows," Iris—quote/unquote Iris—answered Lara.

I wriggled out from under the pew, then felt around for whatever had sliced into me. A blast of cool, moist air enveloped my fingers. Yes! I'd just found the fog machine. I switched it off and kept feeling around.

"Someone here knows and is not—"

I felt something else strapped under the pew. I punched a couple of buttons, and Iris's voice cut off.

"Why'd she stop?" asked Robert.

"She's fading," Joe called out.

But I hadn't found any kind of video recorder. And what would the image have been projected on?

Then I got it. The mist. The image had been projected onto the mist. The mist was basically being used as the movie screen. I knew that would work with holograms. That's why *Iris* was fading! The mist was breaking up!

I stood up and waved my arms to get rid of the mist faster. "I just found a fog machine and a tape recorder," I announced. "Ten bucks to the person who finds the holographic camera first."

Lara scrambled to her feet. "What are you talking about?" she demanded.

"He's saying the whole thing is a fake," Harlan answered. He got up and hit the lights. "Nice job, Lara. You fooled me, and I'm the expert prank player."

"You think I set this up?" she exclaimed.

"Who else? The séance was your idea," said Cyndi.

"Who else?" Lara shot back. "Any of you. You all had time to set this up." She whirled to face Harlan. "And like you said, you're the expert prank player."

"I didn't even know where the séance was going to be the first night," Harlan protested. "I'm good, but I'm not that good."

"I told you," Lara insisted. "I told you the chapel. When we were talking about the séance, I said that the chapel would be the safest place to contact a spirit." She looked over at Robert. "You were there, remember?"

"She did say that in front of us, dude," Robert said, sounding a little apologetic.

"We're all getting kind of loud here," Joe commented. He was wandering around behind the altar.

"Okay, so maybe you said it in front of us," Harlan hissed at Lara. "Who knows how many other people you told?"

"I don't know why anybody would think it was a fun prank to make me think Iris was back from the grave to kill me," said Cyndi.

"Iris never said it was your blood she was talking about," Lara told her. "You must have a seriously guilty conscience."

"Iris never said anything," I reminded them. "Iris is dead. Everything you heard came from that tape recorder under the pew."

"And you put it there, Lara. Just admit it," Cyndi insisted. I had to agree that Lara was definitely a suspect for creating Iris's ghost.

SUSPECT PROFILE

Name: Lara Renner

Hometown: New York, New York

Physical description: 5'5", 130 lbs., age 16, blond hair, blue eyes.

Occupation: Student/sentenced to Undercliff.

Background: Middle child. Father a multimedia artist. Mother deceased.

Suspicious behavior: Set up séances to contact Moses and Iris.

Suspected of: Faking hauntings at Undercliff.

Possible motive: To convince people that ghosts exist.

The problem was, Lara had arrived at Undercliff the same day Joe and I had. A lot of the badness that had occurred at Undercliff had happened before she'd ever shown up. Unless she'd managed to find ways to sneak into the detention center before she was sentenced here . . .

"You owe me ten bucks, Frank," Joe told me. He'd circled around behind me and was holding up a video camera. It looked pretty standard, but it was obviously extremely high-tech.

"Can I get a look at that?" Harlan asked.

Joe shrugged. Letting suspects mess with evidence is not something any detective would let happen. But we couldn't act like detectives.

Harlan took the camera out of Joe's hands. "You didn't used to be able to shoot holograms without using lasers to illuminate the objects. That was obviously completely limiting."

"Obviously," Robert muttered.

"But now you can film in regular light and convert the images digitally." Harlan shook his head. "Pretty awesome that you can project them with something as basic as this."

"He sounds like he knows an awful lot about it, doesn't he?" Lara asked, staring at Harlan.

"Your dad probably does too," Cyndi jumped in. "He's this famous multimedia artist guy, right?" She didn't wait for an answer. "Multimedia, that could include movies. And I bet holograms, too."

"It does. But so what?" asked Lara. "You think my dad had holographic film footage of some girl I'd never even heard of before I got here just lying around his studio? Which I just happened to decide to bring with me for my Undercliff vacation?"

"You knew her. You were here at the same time she was," Cyndi said to Harlan.

"I can't exactly afford this kind of equipment," Harlan told her.

Lara raised her eyebrows. "Yeah, none of us at Undercliff would ever consider stealing anything."

She had a point.

"I don't know about the rest of you, but I'm getting out of here," Joe told the group. "With the amount of noise we've been making, somebody's going to come and check things out. And I'm not climbing out the window to save your behinds this time."

He was right. We weren't going to find out anything else right now. We'd just hear a bunch more accusations and counteraccusations.

"I'm out too," I said. "We should go one at a time. We're less likely to get caught that way."

Harlan left the chapel without a word. I noticed he hadn't put down the camera.

I waited half a minute, then followed him, moving fast. I picked the lock of the door leading to the back stairs. I wanted to beat Harlan back to the dorm so I could see if he'd stash the camera or examine it or trash it. It might give me and Joe a little extra info to work with.

I opened the door leading to the second floor. The hallway was dark and silent. I took a step out, and somebody grabbed me by the elbow.

I was hoping it was Joe, the way it had been the last time. I was really, really hoping it was Joe.

I glanced over my shoulder.

It wasn't Joe.

"I think you'd better come with me," Micah said.

Liar!

Frank should be back by now, I thought. *He should have been back before me.* I rolled over on my side in bed and stared through the darkness at the dorm door. *Where is he?*

Okay, this was ridiculous. I wasn't going to lie here like a lump anymore. I threw off the covers and got up. I yanked my jeans back on and jammed my feet back into my sneakers. Frank had probably decided to do a little snooping on the way back from the chapel. Well, he wasn't going to have all the fun. He definitely wasn't going to solve this thing without me.

Besides, he might need backup. Because, truthfully, Frank's not the type to disappear without saying anything. He would have given me a heads-up. He practically gives me a daily itinerary complete with drinking fountain stops when we're on a case.

I headed for the door. "Where are you going?" Robert asked quietly.

"Just want to check on Frank. He probably decided to raid the kitchen on the way back," I answered.

"If you go in there, bring me a doughnut," Harlan whispered.

"Yep." I ducked out the door and tried to figure out the most likely Frank location. Harlan was high on our suspect list, but I couldn't think of any Harlan-related investigating Frank could be doing right now. Lara was definitely a possibility to have staged the two ghost appearances at the séances. But the middle of the night wasn't exactly a prudent time to do a search of the girls' dorm. And Frank was all about the prudent.

I remembered that a new player had been added to our suspect roster tonight. Micah. This actually would be a good time to do some recon on him. The guy worked long hours, but he'd been at the center for a ton of hours. He had to sleep sometime. Which meant his office was probably empty right now.

So I hurried down the hall and into the back stairwell. It creeped me out. I never thought I'd miss peach paint, but I did. The gray stone of the walls and the stairs made me feel like I might have been transported back a few hundred years to the days when Undercliff was an asylum. Why hadn't I remembered to bring a flashlight? Frank never forgot to bring a flashlight!

"Next time, he can come looking for me," I muttered. The sound of my voice just made me realize how quiet the stairway was. I picked up the pace and practically burst out into the first-floor hall.

Not a smart move. I should have checked to make sure the hall was empty. Turned out it was, but I should have checked. I figured Micah's office was probably somewhere near Maggie's mom's, so I turned in that direction.

And you know what I realized? Even peach paint can look kind of spooky when you're by yourself at night in a place that's supposed to be haunted. Even if you and your brother have pretty much proved that the ghosts haunting the place are fakes. Yeah, Playback, I know. Wimp, wimp, wimp!

Micah's office turned out to be two down from Dr. Nosek's. I tried the door. Locked. Not a problem. I picked the lock and stepped inside. No Frank. But since I was in here, I figured I should look around a little. Get whatever info there was to be gotten.

The blinds were drawn, so I figured it was safe to turn on the small desk lamp. And since I was over by the desk, I decided to start there. Center drawer. The usual stuff—Post-its, pens (all with chewed ends), pencils, some change, a ruler, tape, paper clips, yadda, yadda, yadda.

Top side drawer. Also basic. Disks, an iPod, an apple, some notepads—I flipped through these to see if there was any juicy stuff, but nope—gloves, a day planner—flipped through that, too—deodorant, gum, mints. Huh, seemed like maybe Micah had odor issues. Also, he wasn't exactly obsessively organized. But nothing in the drawer screamed, or even whispered, killer.

The next drawer down was filled with hanging green file folders. They all had little label tabs on them. But they weren't in alphabetical order or anything. Clearly, Micah fell a lot closer to the Joe side of the Joe/Frank Scale o' Neatness.

I chose the folder that seemed most interesting—the one labeled PERSONAL. And score! Inside was a copy of a letter from Dr. Elton Beirly to—wait for it—Micah's parole officer. Yeah, you heard me. I said parole officer.

Let me pause here for a public-service-type

announcement. If you have papers that are really personal, you know, *private* personal, don't put them in a folder marked PERSONAL. It's the first place a detective, or pretty much your basic nosy person, will look.

The letter was a review of Micah's work. I gave it a quick read. "Excellent time management." "Good motivation." "Its my opinion he's made real progress." "Especially sensitive dealing with the imaginary friend of one of the kids."

I was surprised a doctor didn't have correct apostrophe usage down. But that wasn't the most interesting thing about the letter. Obviously, Beirly had a lot more power over Micah than the average boss did over the average employee. He could do a lot more than fire Micah. If he wrote some seriously bad stuff, he might even be able to get Micah's parole revoked. No wonder Micah was willing to get his dry cleaning. It definitely explained why Beirly told Micah that he had to be a good boy and follow orders.

I needed to talk over the Beirly/Micah situation with Frank. I bet he would have some ideas. Of course, I had to find him first. Where was he? I was so sure he'd be right here in Micah's office.

I promised myself I'd finish the office search ASAP and get back to the brother search. There was nothing else interesting in the personal file. Some bank statements with no unusually big deposits or withdrawals. A reminder notice from the dentist. From his personal file, Micah didn't seem to have much of a personal life going.

The file behind the one marked PERSONAL was labeled HEALTH INSURANCE FORMS. Didn't seem like there would be anything relating to the case in that one. But it was really thick. The fattest file in the drawer. And that made me curious.

I looked inside, and there were no forms of any kind. Instead there were copies of the files for Maryama Soll, Gregory Teeter, and Iris Edwards. Holy guacamole! *Ka-ching!* Micah was moving his way up on the Hardy Boy suspect chart.

I decided to start with Iris's file, since Frank and I knew the least about her. The first few pages were her answers to Beirly's initial interview questions. Next up, her police report. She'd been sentenced to Undercliff after several counts of petty larceny. Then weekly reports from Dr. Nosek, who'd been her assigned therapist. I skimmed them. Nothing leaped out at me. Nosek seemed to think Iris was depressed and angry after her parents' divorce and was "acting out." Nothing indicating that Nosek suspected Iris was suicidal.

At the back of the file were copies of some artwork

Iris had done. Some pencil sketches. Not bad. Not that I'm an art expert. And a collage made of family photos. There were comments written around them in marker. *Me, Mom, and Dad at the beach. Aunt Becky at Nathan's b-day party. Cousin Lara and me at Vasona Park.*

Lara. My eyes shot to that picture. It was Lara. *Lara* Lara. Lara was Iris's cousin!

This was so wrong. Lara had acted like she had no idea who Iris even was. She'd been lying to everyone since minute one.

Fight or Flight

I paced around the small room. There wasn't much space to walk. I could make a small U around the three sides of the bed that weren't touching the wall. For a break, I could take an alternate route that would take me into the tiny bathroom.

Relax, I told myself. *Spending the night in the infirmary is no biggie.* In a way it was almost nicer than the dorm. Yeah, the rooms were small, but they were private. That was kind of cool.

I flopped back on the bed. It was pointless to try to break out for two reasons. One: Micah put me in here for the night. Sneaking back out would just get me labeled as a troublemaker. It might limit my freedom to move around the detention center, which would make it harder to complete the investigation.

And two: There was a large mirror over the bed, and I was almost positive it was two-way. Micah could be watching me right now. If he was, breaking out would be impossible. If I tried, he'd just walk in and stop me.

So the logical thing to do was sleep. I untied my sneakers and pulled them off, then got under the covers and closed my eyes. *Sleep,* I told myself. Yeah, right.

Go over the case, I told myself. That I could do.

I was having trouble with the two "ghosts." Why had the ghost of Iris been added to the mix? The Moses ghost was doing everything I figured the haunter-killer wanted it to. Why come up with a whole new—

The sound of someone whimpering yanked me out of my thoughts. The whimpering was definitely coming from inside my room. And I was definitely the only one inside the tiny space. And finally, the whimpering definitely wasn't coming from me.

My muscles tightened. Part of the basic fight-or-flight reaction.

Not a ghost, I told myself. I know, I know, I've been telling myself stuff a lot. But being locked in a little room when there is probably a killer some-where in the building does that to me.

My muscles relaxed a little. See, when you're exposed to a frightening stimulus, the thalamus—the part of the brain that receives sensory input—doesn't know if there is actual danger or not. So it shoots the info to the amygdala through neural impulses. The amygdala wants to protect you, no matter what, so it gets the info to the hypothala-mus, and that part of the brain kicks in the body's fight-or-flight response. That makes you ready to do whatever you've got to do to save your life.

But at the same time, your brain is going through another process. You get hit with the scary stimu-lus and the thalamus also gets the hippocampus and the sensory cortex involved. The hippocampus is the part of the brain that establishes context. It—

 JOE

Joe here. Frank, I realize this is your section, but come on, my brother. Not the time for a science lesson.

 FRANK

I was just trying to explain that my fight-or-flight instinct kicked in because while the hippocam-pus was coming up with the explanations like tape recorders, my amygdala had already sent my body into high alert.

 JOE

Right. Or it could be that you're just a wimp, wimp, wimp!

 FRANK

Joe—

 JOE

Don't bother to say it. I'm leaving. I'm outta here. I'm gone.

FRANK

Anyway, like I was saying, I almost immediately realized that I was being punk'd. Somebody was trying to make me think this room was haunted.

Well, if anyone did happen to be watching from that mirror I was pretty sure was two-way, they'd realize I wasn't having any of it. I got out of bed and began to search the room, slowly and deliberately. There had to be a tape recorder, or CD player, or speakers, or *something*, somewhere close by.

"You fastened them too tight," a voice called. "Let me up, please. I promise I'll be good."

I flashed on what Harlan had said about feeling

restraints wrap around him while he was staying in the infirmary. Then I heard what sounded like someone fighting against restraints. "Please. Please," cried the voice.

I headed toward the bathroom to search in there. I realized my legs were feeling heavy. Arms too.

Don't let this show mess with your mind, I told myself. I *know*. I couldn't stop doing it.

I took another step. Tried to. But I couldn't lift up my foot. My legs—they were so heavy. My whole body was . . . heavy.

Then I was on the floor, without even realizing I was falling. I tried to lift my head. Couldn't.

"Let me up," the voice begged. "I'll be good. I'll be so good."

How was this happening? I sucked in a deep breath. At least my lungs and heart weren't paralyzed.

A sickly sweet smell hit my nose. My hippocampus struggled for context. Anesthesia. I was breathing in anesthesia. Nitrous oxide and something like sevoflurane, probably. Fast-acting and—

This really wasn't the time to analyze it all. If I breathed in too much of whatever the combo was, I could end up in a lot worse shape than I was already in. I could end up dead.

JOE

I opened the door to the girls' dorm. It was against the rules for a guy to be in here. But hey, it's wrong to lie, too. And I wanted to know exactly why Lara had been lying practically every time she opened her mouth.

I scanned the room. My eyes were already pretty adjusted to the dark—since I'd been wandering around without a flashlight. It didn't take too long to spot Lara's blond head poking out from under the covers of one of the beds.

I crept over and pressed my hand over her mouth. I didn't want her to yell and wake everybody up. Her eyes snapped open. "We need to talk. Now," I whispered in her ear. "Out in the hall."

Lara looked at me like I was nutzoid. She also looked like she had no intention of going anywhere with someone who was nutzoid. "What we need to talk about is Iris. *Cousin* Iris."

Lara gave a sharp nod. I slowly took my hand off her mouth. "Let's go," she whispered. She climbed out of bed and walked into the hallway without looking back. "What do you want now?" she asked when I joined her and shut the dorm door behind me.

I didn't have time for this. "Iris Edwards is your cousin. You've been acting like you never heard of her. Why?"

"What business is it of yours?" she demanded.

Was she serious? "You made it my business. You invited me to your séances, remember? What have you been trying to pull?"

"I've been trying to find out who killed my cousin!" Lara blurted out.

"Wait. I thought Iris killed herself," I said.

"No way. There is no way Iris would ever do that," Lara answered. "She was freaked about all the bad stuff happening at Undercliff. About the deaths. She was getting close to finding something out, and someone killed her before she could. I'm positive."

"So that's why you're here?" My gray matter felt like it was crackling.

"I burned down an abandoned barn. I was really careful about it. I was right there the whole time, watching so the fire didn't spread. I was hoping I'd get sent here. It was a long shot. It was stupid. But I had to find out what happened to Iris. I wasn't going to let someone get away with murdering her," Lara said in a rush.

"And you set up the séances to get a confession?" I asked.

"Or just information," she answered. "I figured the séances would get people talking about Iris. Thinking about how she died. I thought if I put it in people's heads that she was murdered, they might remember something that would help me."

It was actually a pretty clever plan.

"My dad had taken some holographic film of Iris. He'd made some real breakthroughs in the technique. Anyway, the holograms of Iris gave me the idea. That, and I knew that everybody thought there were ghosts at Undercliff," Lara continued. "Even Iris."

"Why do you think that?"

"She told me. In letters," Lara explained. "She even found some pages from Moses's journal." She pulled a couple of sheets of yellowed paper from the pocket of her pajama bottoms and handed them to me. "I always keep them with me. She sent them to me in her last letter."

I began to read.

Summer 1810
I no longer know the month. I believe the year is still 1810, but Im not certain. I know my name is Moses Bottelle. I know I will not scream. I know I am insane. Sane. I know I am sane. I do not hear imaginary voices. I am not possessed by demons. I do not wish to do harm to anyone. I only wish to leave this place. My name is Moses Bottelle.

Today the doctor brought me what he considered good news. He is going to try a different treatment with me. It is called the spinning chair. I will be put in the chair and spun until the humors within my brain separate. The doctor has explained that an excess of one of these humors, black bile, yellow bile, blood, or phlegm, is causing my madness. Separating the humors will allow them to become correctly balanced once again.

I have seen two others who have been treated in the spinning chair. I have seen blood dripping from their ears when they were returned to their cells. And more than this, I saw all logic stripped from them. They did not know familiar faces, and much more frightening, they did not seem to know themselves.

This may be the last journal entry I write. This may be the last time that I am able to think about that sunrise, that walk, that nest and bird, that meal and game of chess. This may be the last time Im able to remember the names of my dogs, Posey, Jimmy, and Red. This may be the last time that I'll know a woman named Charlotte once loved me, and that I loved her. This may be the last time

I am able to understand that I am Moses Bottelle.
This may be the last day I can call myself sane.

I pray that I will not scream.

When I finished the journal entry, I looked up Lara. "I know who the killer is."

FRANK

19

Exploding Head

Fresh air. That's what I needed. Fresh air. But there was no window in my little room. Options. There had to be other options. There always were if you thought long enough.

Except I might not have that long. The anesthesia would knock me out pretty soon. Or kill me if somebody wasn't monitoring me pretty closely.

Monitoring. The two-way mirror. There'd be fresh air on the other side. If it was a two-way.

I needed to break it. Maybe I could grab the desk chair and—

And what? I couldn't move. I couldn't lift one finger. Forget about a chair.

"Help!" I yelled. "Let me out of here!"

"Let me up!" the ghostly voice cried. "Don't leave me in here. Please!"

Did anybody hear us?

 JOE

"You know who killed Iris?" Lara exclaimed. "Who?"

"I'm not sure about Iris," I admitted. "But I'm almost positive Dr. Beirly killed Maryama Soll and Gregory Teeter."

"If Iris found that out, Beirly would have killed her, too," said Lara. "But why do you think it's Beirly?"

"Because Beirly messes up on when to use an apostrophe, and so does the person who wrote this journal entry," I explained.

"Moses Bottelle wrote the journal entry," Lara reminded me, all impatience. "Hundreds of years ago."

"There never was a Moses Bottelle at the Undercliff Asylum," I corrected her. "I found a list of all the patients on the Net. He wasn't on it. Somebody created Bottelle. Beirly. He's the one. He created Bottelle to make all the ghost stuff at Undercliff seem more convincing. And sometimes the haunting went bad and people died. I don't know if Beirly meant for it to happen or not. But it did."

"Why would he haunt his own detention center?" Lara protested.

"I don't know. And right this second, I don't care. My brother didn't come back to the dorm after the séance," I told her. "I know Beirly was here late tonight. All I care about right now is making sure Beirly isn't doing anything to hurt Frank."

"Let's split up and look for him," Lara suggested.

"You don't have to do that. I'll find Frank. You can just go back in the dorm," I said.

"If I did that, Iris really would come back from the grave and haunt me. I'll start on the first floor."

"I'm going up to the third. I want to check Beirly's office first," I told her.

"If I find anything, I'll come get you." Lara raced for the back stairs.

I took the main staircase up to the third floor, keeping to the deep shadows near the railing. Then I rushed down the hall and into Beirly's outer office. Empty. The inner office was empty too.

I turned around and through the outer office to the hall. I stopped when I saw the chair I'd sat in the first day. The day I thought I'd discovered a cold spot in this room.

I remembered seeing similar chairs in the storage room with the upholstery removed. That gave me an idea, and I decided to take a few moments to check it out. I yanked my Swiss Army knife from my pocket and sliced into the chair's upholstery. There were coolant coils in the padding underneath.

Well, that was one little mystery solved. Let Beirly freak if he saw the destroyed chair. Let him know somebody was very close to finding out all his secrets.

I went out into the hall and began checking every room. I hit the jackpot when I opened the door to the nurse's office. Beirly sat at the nurse's desk, back to me, typing away at his laptop.

And watching my brother through a two-way window! Watching Frank lie crumpled on the floor of a little room. It was like Beirly was examining a lab rat in a cage.

I had to get Frank out of there. I let out a roar and charged at the door between the nurse's office and the infirmary. Beirly moved faster than I thought he'd be able to for such a doughy guy, and blocked me. I slammed into him, and it was like running into a redwood. A redwood covered in a layer of fat.

"There's an extremely important experiment going on inside that room," Beirly told me. "We don't want to interrupt."

"That's a human being in there," I shouted. "Not an experiment. Is he even breathing?"

"Calm down," Beirly said. "If you can't, I'll help

you." He reached out and picked up a syringe from the nurse's desk.

I froze and shut my mouth. I wasn't going to be able to help Frank pumped full of sedatives or whatever was in the needle Beirly was holding.

Slowly I raised my hands. "I'm calm. I'm calm. See, I'm calm." I backed away and sat down in the chair on the other side of the desk. "So experiments, huh? Your father was a research scientist, right? Nobel prize and all that."

I talk when I'm nervous. Obviously.

Beirly snorted. "All he did was add a tiny bit to all the work that had been done before him," he said. "My research is completely original."

I shot a fast look through the two-way glass. Frank was so still. I had to get in there. I decided just to keep Beirly talking while I tried to figure out a way.

"Original, huh? Isn't most research built on previous scientific discoveries?" I asked. I slid my eyes across the desk, looking for another syringe. That would even things up a little.

Nada.

"My theory is completely unique," Beirly answered. "I've come up with a connection between the strength of a juvenile's fear response and the likelihood that a juvenile will commit a crime. The less fear a juvenile expresses in a situation where fear is appropriate, the more likely it is that he—or she—will engage in criminal behavior."

"So that's why you asked all those questions when I first got here. About scary movies and roller coasters and bungee jumping and all that."

"Exactly. I was trying to get an initial reading on your fear response. The more a juvenile enjoys thrill-seeking activities, the lower the fear response." Beirly sounded happy I'd caught on so fast.

I hoped he hadn't realized exactly how much I'd caught on to. I hoped my next question would surprise him—and give me the chance to take action. "So that's why you created the ghost of Moses Bottelle. To test kids' fear response. That's why you killed Maryama and Gregory."

Beirly's face went red. "I didn't intend to kill—"

I didn't wait to hear his lame excuses. I leaped to my feet, grabbed the chair in front of the nurse's desk, and swung it at Beirly's head. It hit with a meaty thump, and Beirly swayed on his feet, then went down.

I scrambled over his back and through the door into the infirmary. There were three individual patient rooms. Frank was in the second one. I dropped down next to him. His breathing was shallow, but he was breathing.

"Air," Frank said, so softly I almost didn't hear him. "Need air."

I realized that the air in the room did smell weird. Sweet and nauseating. I grabbed Frank by the shoulders and hauled him out into the main infirmary room. Then I opened every window in sight.

"I'll be right back," I told Frank. "I just have to finish up something."

I ran back to the nurse's office. Beirly had made it up to his knees, but he still looked dazed. The first thing I did was liberate the syringe he had in his hand. "You're going to be a good boy, and do what I tell you," I said. "Or I'm injecting this into you. Whatever it is."

"I didn't mean to kill anyone," Beirly said, his words a little slurred.

"Right. Then why didn't you stop your experiments after Gregory died?" I demanded as I lashed his hands together behind his back with Ace bandages.

"I thought I'd corrected the error in the chemical mix he inhaled," he told me.

"And what about Iris?" Lara stepped into the room, eyes on fire. "That wasn't an error."

"I couldn't let her go to the police." Beirly blinked several times. "I needed more data. Enough to publish a paper. Enough to show my father that I was so much more than he—"

"I've heard enough, have you?" I asked Lara. She nodded, and I used another bandage to gag Beirly.

I picked the phone up from the nurse's desk. "You want to make the call?" I asked.

Lara smiled. "So much." She dialed 911. "This is for you, Iris."

 FRANK

"Beirly's coming out," I said. I gripped the sill of the open infirmary window with both hands. I was still feeling a little queasy, but the paralysis had disappeared from my body.

"You left out the most important part," Lara told me. "Beirly's coming out in handcuffs. What do you think they're waiting for?"

"They're probably arresting Micah, too," Joe commented.

"They should," I said. "He knew everything that was going on. Probably that psychic Beirly used too. Or if she didn't know everything, she at least had been hired to give out exactly the information Beirly wanted revealed."

"I think he wanted to stop it. Beirly just had him on a short leash. One word from Beirly and Micah would go back to jail," Joe pointed out.

"Now he's going anyway," said Lara. "Look, he's coming out the door. In handcuffs. He should have shown some guts. He could have stopped this whole thing. Iris would be alive right now, if Micah had stepped up."

"Or if Beirly hadn't turned out to be a complete sociopath." Joe glanced down. "Hey, your feet must be freezing without your bunny slippers, Lara."

She gave a short laugh. "I hate those things. I only wore them to the séance because they were loose enough that I could fit the remote control for the tape recorder in the toes."

All the details were coming clear. "You knew what 'Iris' was going to say. But you still needed to control when she said it."

"Yeah. I told everyone I had to be the only one to talk to the spirit, but I still didn't think I could time my questions perfectly with so many other people around. That's why I had to use a remote," Lara explained.

"The fog machine and camera?" Joe asked.

"Timers," she said.

"They're leaving," I announced.

We watched in silence as four police officers escorted Beirly and Micah across Undercliff's wide front lawn and then loaded them into a squad car.

"Iris . . . ," Lara breathed.

"You found her killer," I said.

"Iris," Lara said more loudly.

"You did what you came here to do," Joe told her. "You were awesome."

"Iris," Lara said again.

Joe and I looked at each other. Neither of us knew what to say next.

Lara pointed down at the lawn. "Iris!" she cried. "Look! Iris!"

"No way," Joe mumbled.

I staggered back a step. I'm sure I was still feeling the side effects of the anesthesia. Then I got it together. I turned to Lara. "So where's the camera this time?" I asked.

"I'm not doing this!" she exclaimed. "It's really Iris." She had tears in her eyes.

Not acceptable. If she wasn't going to tell me, I was going to find out for myself. I headed for the door as fast as I could. Which wasn't very fast.

"Where are you going?" Joe called after me.

"To find the camera!" I answered. I got down to the first floor as fast as I could. Which wasn't very fast. I didn't want anyone to have time to move that camera.

"There's no camera, Frank," Lara protested—the way she had been all the way down the stairs. "I didn't do anything this time," she said as she and Joe followed me out the front door.

Iris still stood on the front lawn. The projected

image of Iris, I mean. "I'm going to find it," I told Lara. "You might as well just tell me where it is."

But Lara was just staring at the glowing image of her cousin. "She looks so happy."

As if Iris had heard, she turned toward us. And she smiled, this huge smile. Her image brightened and brightened until I had to shut my eyes. When I opened them, she—the projected image of her, I mean—was gone.

I took my small, high-power flashlight out of my pocket and began to shine it up in the nearby trees.

"Frank, there's no mist out here," Joe said.

"That makes it easier to see," I answered, slowly moving the beam from branch to branch.

"There's no concave mirror, either," Joe went on.

"My dad made some big improvements in holographic technology," Lara added. "But his holograms still need a screen."

The flashlight fell out of my fingers. I got what they were saying. A hologram has to be projected onto *something*. Iris's image had been projected onto the mist during the séances. But there was no mist out on the lawn. No concave mirror—another type of screen that can be used with holograms.

All there was where Iris had been was an empty stretch of lawn. I walked forward and ran my fingers over the grass where I'd seen her standing. Just normal grass, soft and a little dewy.

"I—I—this can't—," I stammered.

"Step back," Joe warned Lara, his voice a little shaky. "My brother's head is about to explode."

 JOE

"So how was the scenery?" Mom asked as soon as Frank and I walked in the door. "Was it worth the trip to Connecticut?" The whole family had trooped into the entry hall to greet us.

"Frank almost fainted. That's how awesome the scenery was," I told her.

"I can imagine. The fall leaves are really extraordinary at this time of the year," Aunt Trudy commented. "You boys should have volunteered me as a chaperone. I would have loved to go on that trip."

"Next time, Aunt T," I promised.

I tried to imagine our aunt on an ATAC mission. Actually, she'd probably kick tail. Definitely if she'd caught Beirly using Frank to experiment on, she would have taken him downtown. All by herself. Well, maybe she would have had to break out one of those Jell-O salads she makes in the shape of a fish. Those things weigh a ton.

"What did you do for Halloween?" Dad asked. "I've heard there are some haunted spots near Glastonbury that are popular for parties on All Hallows Eve."

That Dad. He's a funny guy, right? He knew exactly what our mission was. And by now I'm sure he knew exactly how it had turned out.

"Frank was too exhausted from experiencing the wonder of the fall leaves to go out," I answered.

"Actually, I just let him think that," said Frank. "I knew Joe was afraid of seeing one of those ghosts you were talking about, so I gave him an excuse to lock himself in the hotel."

"Wimp, wimp, wimp!" Playback called from the kitchen.

"And proud of it," I agreed.

PENDRAGON

Bobby Pendragon is a seemingly normal fourteen-year-old boy. He has a family, a home, and a possible new girlfriend. But something happens to Bobby that changes his life forever.

HE IS CHOSEN TO DETERMINE
THE COURSE OF HUMAN EXISTENCE.

Pulled away from the comfort of his family and suburban home, Bobby is launched into the middle of an immense, interdimensional conflict involving racial tensions, threatened ecosystems, and more. It's a journey of danger and discovery for Bobby, and his success or failure will do nothing less than determine the fate of the world. . . .

Coming Soon: Book Eight: *The Pilgrims of Rayne*

From Aladdin Paperbacks • Published by Simon & Schuster

Looking for a great read?

MARGARET PETERSON HADDIX